I0629166

Margaret in Moscow

Also by R. L. Rhyse

Margaret of Greenwich - Margaret and Erika

Margaret at War - Margaret in Tokyo

Margaret and Eve - Margaret and Velda

Margaret and Emily - Margaret and Hillary

Margaret in London - Margaret at Barnard

Margaret at Barnard/Part Two: Deliverance

Margaret in Berlin – Margaret in Manhattan

Margaret and Venla – Margaret: Mother of Twins

R. L. Rhyse

Margaret in Moscow
Book Sixteen in the
Margaret of Greenwich® Series

Wyston Books, Inc.

MARGARET IN MOSCOW

Wyston Books, Inc.

www.magaretofgreenwich.com

www.wystonbooks.com

This is a work of fiction. All names, characters, places, and incidents are the product of the author's imagination or used fictitiously. Any resemblance to actual events, locations, or persons, living or dead, is entirely coincidental.

Margaret in Moscow: a novel

Book Sixteen in the Margaret of Greenwich® Series

1.   Margaret of Greenwich (Fictitious character)
2.   Teenage Girls Fiction

Library of Congress Control Number: 2019947800
ISBN 978-0-9991057-4-0
eISBN 978-0-9991057-5-7

Cover Photo by JamesBrey/Licensed from Getty Images

BISAC: YAF022000 (Girls & Women) - YAF011000 (Coming of Age) - YAF029000 (Law & Crime)

MARGARET IN MOSCOW

Being insane is not critical to working undercover but it helps.

–Margaret

MARGARET IN MOSCOW

Chapter 1

It is four years since I last picked up my pen, as diarists say, and my twins' fourth birthday approached. "You're too old to carry," I said, and picked them up. A mother's behavior isn't always rational.

James and Donna don't yet have a live-in daddy. Randy, their father, is a Ph.D. student in Computer Science at Columbia University. He lives in an apartment on West One-Hundred-Thirteenth Street, a short walk from school. When we'll marry is our continuing disagreement.

"You can't push him into marriage even if he is your children's father and you've dated since high school," Erika said.

We're like sisters so I take her advice seriously.

"I'm angry!" I burst out.

"That's because you're frustrated. You must accept that while he loves you and will almost certainly marry you, he's not yet grown-up. Maybe when he gets his doctorate," Erika said cheerfully, with a smile.

"You're right. I'm not seeing things as they are," I said, with a sigh.

"It's harder when dealing with men," Erika said firmly.

This position got no argument from me.

"So what else is happening?" Erika asked, wanting to change the subject to something productive.

"The children's birthday party on Saturday. Vladimir and Borya will be here," I said.

"Not just for that, I expect. For those heavyweights to come, something big must be happening," Erika said.

I was about to speak when Donna screamed that James grabbed her toy.

Chapter 2

Vladimir and Borya lead different lives. Vladimir is a retired general of Russia's Presidential Security Service and directs a private security firm in Berlin. Borya is a general in Russia's Military Intelligence Service, the SVR (*Sluzhba Vneshney Razvedki*), which is responsible for intelligence from Europe and the Western Hemisphere. Vladimir served heroically in Russia's Afghanistan military misadventure; Borya's son, a Russian Air Force flyer, was killed in Syria.

My relationship with them is complex. My biological mother, Lena, had concurrent affairs with Vladimir and Peter, a British Secret Intelligence Service (SIS) agent. Because a DNA test was never performed, each considers me their daughter. This could easily have led to problems but they wound up as business partners and both love me. We are just another of the unconventional family structures existing today. I work in their business and we have frequent contact though Peter lives in London and Vladimir lives in Berlin.

Vladimir, Peter, and Borya join forces when national interests coincide. Thanks to their efforts, a bio-terror attack on West Point had been smashed. This also led to the rescue of my twin brother, Creighton, who I had never met. It was a big day for everyone.

While soothing Donna's feelings and telling James that it wasn't nice to grab his sister's toy, I wondered what was going on. Not that I didn't welcome their visit and the children the elaborate presents they always brought, but would a brewing crisis involve me?

"Uncle Vladimir and Uncle Borya are coming!" I exclaimed cheerily.

The children instantly froze and grinned.

"Aren't we lucky!" I added, in the exaggerated tone that captures young children's attention.

I hoped.

Chapter 3

Vladimir and Borya arrived at Newark Airport on a private flight from Berlin. They were driven to Greenwich in a limousine bearing small Russian flags. Because my bedrooms were filled, Erika offered to put them up in her family's forty-million-dollar mansion.

"The guards speak Russian so they'll feel at home," she said.

While this was true, I wondered if her billionaire father's business interests were a factor though he enjoys diverting company which Vladimir and Borya certainly are.

They didn't visit me until late the following morning, a good time since by then my babies were fed. Though their breast feeding period was over, they still occasionally grabbed for my breasts and in public too. I don't often turn red but did then.

Their uncles' arrival was a happy occasion but their gifts were too mature for toddlers. One, the Little Tikes STEM Jr. Wonder Lab Toy, included twenty experiments in Science, Technology, Engineering, and Math with playful sounds. Likely, most play would simply be throwing the balls that it included.

Because of my motherly obsession with cleanliness, after reading in the instructions that one of the experiments created stretchy slime, I planned to ditch this toy as soon as their uncles left.

The Mega Blocks Scooping Wagon, which picked up small blocks scattered on the floor, was more to my liking though I praised both gifts.

"*Aren't these wonderful!*" I gushed, as the kids jumped up and down before running to hug the givers.

These jolly family moments lasted until Mila, our family bodyguard, wheedled the kids with their new toys from the room. Vladimir immediately turned toward me.

"We must talk," he said in a serious tone, as Borya moved closer.

Chapter 4

"How friendly were you with Page?" Borya asked.

I startled, as if being abruptly awakened from a nightmare. I hadn't heard her name in three years.

Page was both gorgeous elegant call girl and assassin. When I last heard, she was employed by Russia though she might have switched employer since her talents are widely appreciated.

Our relationship was as deceitful as her work. A mysterious death in Russia's Berlin consulate convulsed Europe and I was tasked to help discover what happened. By adopting the role of call girl, I had lived with Page and we became buddies after a fashion. In a spur-of-the-moment burst of creative fiction, I told her that I had killed both my sexually abusive father and a customer who tried to stiff me. After describing her role in the consulate assassination, she and her boss were arrested.

While awaiting trial, he was murdered on a Berlin street, tearful innocence-convincing Page changed employer, and I returned to being a mother. Having never learned my true identity, Page continued to consider me her twin though not with looks since she is an eleven on a scale of one to ten.

"She trusted me," I told Borya, with a shrug.

Borya looked at Vladimir.

"We need you to live with her again," Vladimir said.

I burst out laughing. Their request seemed crazy.

"You want me to live with her?" I asked, astonished.

"Yes, for a short time."

"Where? In Moscow?"

"Yes."

Being an unmarried mother of toddlers, emotions boiled within but, controlling myself, I only asked, "Why?"

Chapter 5

Though a grown-up, I felt myself a child being directed by adults. Which isn't surprising since both Vladimir and Borya were tough. Borya asked, "What's your opinion of Page?"

My answer couldn't be simple since I both liked and loathed her. She was like a friend whose nature repulses as it overpowers. They noted my troubled expression and waited. Finally, I spoke.

"She's a warped person with serious emotional problems and a psychopathic element that lets her avoid adult responsibility. Maybe still seeking revenge for the terrible things done to her. We became close as my fictional killings fed her resentments, murder being her payback."

"That's a sound analysis," Vladimir said, as Borya nodded agreement.

Their praise pleased me. Though experienced through earlier covert operations, I felt myself a beginner in the profession of spying. Buoyed by their approval, I repeated my question, "Why do you want me to live with her?" The answer came in a roundabout way.

"What is the greatest possible national catastrophe?" Borya asked.

"War," I said quickly, considering this answer obvious.

"Why do nations go to war? Apart from those with mad leaders like Hitler or Mao?" Borya asked.

Being Russian, he didn't include Stalin amongst the crazed leaders but I didn't say this.

"Because of national economic interests. Like when Japan believed that attacking America was their only alternative after we stopped selling them oil in 1941," I answered quickly.

"Or?" Borya persisted.

This response was slower in coming.

"Following an act so appalling that a nation considers war their only option. Like after the terror attack on New York's World Trade Center," I suggested.

"Yes. A behavior so incendiary that people demand war. And if a head-of-state is murdered?" Vladimir asked.

I suddenly understood why they were here and felt afraid. All people, especially mothers, fear war.

Chapter 6

"You believe that Page has been hired to murder a head-of-state?" I asked.

"We're not sure," Borya said, slowly.

"She no longer works for you?" I asked, feeling puzzled.

"She does and she doesn't," Borya replied.

He doesn't want to tell this story, I thought.

"As you've gathered, Page isn't stable. But though increasingly unreliable, we couldn't simply let her go. She has an important friend."

I understood yet couldn't help wondering how many other lovers she had.

"You can't let her go," I repeated.

We both knew that letting her go would require she be killed. Page knew too much. Her memoir would be a blockbuster, maybe made into a movie or even a TV series.

"There are political conflicts," Borya said.

"When has there not been?" I asked, in a know-it-all tone. Then adding, "OK, I'll shut," in response to Vladimir's disapproving look. Borya continued.

"Highly placed Russians have taken conflicting sides. Page is rumored involved and to have accepted independent work."

"How do you know this?" I asked, critically.

Borya gave me a kindly look. I should have realized that her phone and car and apartment were bugged. He ignored my question and continued.

"Because of her lover's position, we must have clear evidence before the President will approve action," Borya said.

I knew what that would be.

Chapter 7

I squirmed, wanting to reject their request but feeling unable. They loved me and wouldn't have asked if my involvement weren't vital. And if the outcome might be war, how could I refuse? So I simply asked, "When?"

"Would two days give you enough time to settle things?" Vladimir asked.

"It'll have to," I said, acceptingly.

"Whatever you need will be provided," Borya said.

I rose and hugged each of them.

"Don't worry. It'll work out," I said, with a smile.

The following days went by in a blur. Though Mila, my live-in bodyguard and occasional babysitter, was trustworthy, I arranged for my children to stay with their grandparents. Being their first grandchildren, they are treated like royalty. I told James and Donna that their mother must travel but they would have *lots* of presents when she returned.

That was the easy part. Dealing with their father, Randy, was harder for he had always been a worry-wort. Getting vaccinated terrified him and he had fainted at the sight of blood.

Now he had *real* fears for he need soon defend his doctoral dissertation without my emotional support. My foreign travel would add to his worries. He feared my mugging even when I shopped with my friend, Erika, in Manhattan. This though, being a billionaire's daughter, she doesn't travel without at least one armed bodyguard in an armor-placed SUV. I need maintain phone contact with Randy no matter where I would be, I decided.

"Randy's doctoral exam is coming up and he'll fall apart without having me to talk to. The kids will have a ball staying with my parents but I must be able to speak with them too," I said.

"We can arrange that. Moscow has modern phone service, you know," Borya said, with a smile.

Only then did my looming trip seem real.

Chapter 8

While my parents welcomed their grandchildren's stay, Randy was, as I expected, shattered.

"I need you," he moaned.

"We'll FaceTalk and you won't miss me at all," I said.

`   *"I will, I will,"* he insisted, tearily.

This reassured me since he still hadn't proposed. I feared becoming one of those foolish females who support their boyfriend through his maturing only to pass him on to another woman.

Years earlier in Berlin, using my scheme and Randy's hacking skill, we stole twenty-three million dollars of a crook's ill-gotten gains. My decision to control these funds was seeming increasingly wise.

Having sex often mellows and it did with Randy that day. Afterward, he spoke evenly.

"Where are you going?" he asked.

Since a secret remains secret only if unspoken, I parried his question.

"Abroad but not for long."

"Is it for Borya?"

"Yes."

"Why was Vladimir here?"

"They're brothers. Family is important to Russians and they wanted to see the children," I said.

Randy accepted my lame explanation. Having sex calmed him and I was beginning to feel like the wife who bartered sex to get something.

He soon left, having an early morning meeting with his school advisor the next day. He would sleep in Manhattan that night. I had the scary thought to check on him, fearing that I was becoming a stalking lover. Instead, I stripped and studied my body in the bathroom mirror.

How much had I changed since last meeting Page? Could I still be believable as a whore? Whether from my healthy diet or the effort of caring for twins, I had kept my shape. Well enough to attract stares when not pushing a double stroller, that is.

Chapter 9

Adopting a different identity means becoming another person. While dressing differently can be done quickly, *feeling* like someone else takes time which I didn't have. Thus while mothering and doing chores, I practiced being a whore. Walking with a sexy slink, staring obliquely with an inviting half-smile and saying catchy lines. I created amusing stories about fictional customers to tell Page, speaking them before a mirror to check that my facial expressions matched the words.

I created a phony boyfriend, Raul, to keep Page from fixing me up. That I could convincingly change my identity both reassured and bothered me. While few people get the life they intended, being a whore had never been mine. Nor was abruptly leaving my children.

"How can I tell them?" I moaned to Mila.

A former doctor and Russian Special Forces soldier, she had been assigned as my bodyguard. Being the manager of an international security firm's American office, my safety was important for the company. Both I and my children had become close with Mila and her medical knowledge had kept me from

MARGARET IN MOSCOW

unneeded worry when their normal symptoms cropped up.

"They're smart kids. Say that you must go on a business trip but while mommy is gone, their grandparents and Auntie Mila will make sure they have lots of fun. That should do it," she said.

"What would I do without you?" I gushed.

"The same. You're a good mother. Don't put yourself down," Mila said.

"It's nerves. I haven't worked undercover for years," I said.

"You wouldn't be chosen if you hadn't the ability. It *is* just nerves. You'll be fine once you're there though where I shouldn't ask," Mila said.

"Far away," I said, with a smile which lessened by the moment.

Chapter 10

Despite repeated invitations, I had never been to Moscow. Either it wasn't the right time or my babies were too young. I might have been afraid too.

Each country has a different culture even as American states do. But whereas Americans speak the same language, Russian differs even in alphabet from its European neighbors and is frighteningly huge, extending from the Arctic to Europe.

Yet I had been close with Russians for years. Vladimir, a retired Russian general, considers me a daughter, and Borya, a Russian intelligence official, is my cherished uncle. Moreover, a best friend from college married a doctor whose father is a Russian diplomat.

My journey would be in two stages: a Lufthansa flight to Berlin to consult with Vladimir followed by an Aeroflot flight to Moscow where Borya would advise me. I didn't doubt my need for help from both.

I slept poorly the night before leaving, having been awakened by a nightmare. In it, I was in a barely furnished room with black-painted walls and white-painted luminescent stars glowing on the ceiling. While seated on the bed, I suddenly saw Page lying beside me.

"I was waiting for you," she said, with an inviting smile.

I returned her smile before seeing the dagger in her hand.

Chapter 11

I left early the following morning to avoid having to hug my children goodbye. Fearing their tears and feeling worse if there weren't any. Also feeling nervous but comforted by Vladimir's long-past advice: "Don't fear being afraid. Soldiers who deny it get themselves and others killed."

Though dying young wasn't a preoccupation, I had never denied its possibility. So, though barely twenty when giving birth, I had made a will. Danger was also on my mother's mind when I left. She is a worrier for which I had often given cause.

"Must you go?" she asked, nervously.

"It's critical. Vladimir and Borya practically begged me," I said.

"Can you tell me where you're going?" she pleaded.

"No, but I'll FaceTime regularly and be back before you know it. You'll hardly miss me," I said.

As she attempted a smile, I pushed the previous night's dream from my mind. I quickly hugged goodbye;

more talk would simply make things worse. I grabbed one suitcase, Mila grabbed the other, and we left for the airport.

My best friend, Erika, had wanted to accompany me to the airport but I refused. I needed to get my head on straight, re-adopt my role as Page's buddy and fellow whore and eject other memories. I was no longer no longer a single mother with a tentative fiancée. Instead, I had killed a father who sexually abused me and a customer who tried to stiff me. Both tales impressed Page and I would create others.

"You'll do it," Mila said, as we separated.

I nodded, smiled, and walked toward the departure gate without looking back.

Chapter 12

Berlin has Manhattan's cultural advantages with fewer hassles. My hometown, Greenwich, is good for a family but even its fans admit that it's boring. While more happens there than in the typical suburb where free coffee at a new gas station produces a crowd, Greenwich is far from jumping Manhattan. Berlin has both bustle and livability.

Vladimir met me at the airport. We spoke of family matters until arriving at the apartment building which his family called home. My step-mother, Ulrika, and their daughter nicknamed Beauty, greeted me like the long-unseen family member that I was. Though we spoke frequently on the phone, I hadn't visited Berlin in years.

Memories returned: my initial surprise at learning that Germans bought bread in bread stores, a novelty for Americans whose bread is packaged for supermarket sale; and their elegant Charlottenburg neighborhood. At seven, Beauty had grown even more into her nickname.

"When she's a teenager, you'll have to keep Mace by the door to drive off boys," I said.

"No, German boys aren't American," Ulrika said, with a laugh.

Vladimir rose and kissed Beauty who had been leaning against his chair.

"We must talk, in the office," he said, leading me from the room.

"How are you?" Vladimir asked, once we were seated.

"Fine," I said.

"You don't look it."

"Okay, I'm not fine. Changing mind-frame from mother to whore isn't easy. One slip and it's over," I said.

"You won't slip,"

"I wish I had your confidence."

"Page will remember you as you were and interpret your behavior in that light. She's shallow, not like you."

"But sharp too or she wouldn't have survived this long," I said.

"Survival is often a matter of luck. She won't be so lucky this time," Vladimir said.

Chapter 13

"What's the plan?" I asked.

"You're booked tomorrow on Aeroflot to Moscow. Borya will meet your plane and settle you in. He's assigned you a handler and you're never to be out of her sight," Vladimir said.

I didn't speak for several moments as the import of his words sunk in. While his concern was plain, what he said couldn't happen. There had to be times when Page and I would be alone.

"It's that dangerous?" I asked.

"Moscow has always been a city of intrigues with safety linked to the winning side. But the President is watching and you're Borya's niece. You couldn't be safer," Vladimir said.

Still, he seemed uneasy and I asked, "What's wrong?"

"Page is crazy and I'm not sure you know real craziness," Vladimir said.

"Maybe not but when it's you or them, you tend to choose you and not feel bad about it," I said, with a shrug.

Vladimir smiled and gripped my shoulder.

Being a mother, I hadn't gotten the ironclad safety that I wanted but it would have to do.

"What now?" I asked.

"Now we have dinner with your mother and sister," Vladimir said.

They were really my stepmother and half-sister but our family ties are so muddled that such verbal slips don't count. Our love for each other does.

Being a blended Russian-German family, the usual food combined both cuisines. There is always *borscht*, a beet and cabbage soup which Vladimir prefers with several tablespoons of *smetana*, Russian sour cream. This starter is welcomed by all vegetarians including me. Next came *blini,* a thin crêpe to which Vladimir added a spoonful of black sturgeon caviar, and a Russian salad of cucumber, diced potato, peas, and mayonnaise.

The German dishes also recognized my diet. There was *spätzle* (pasta), asparagus, and whole-grain rye pumpernickel bread. Since meat is the traditional German and Russian dish, I expressed my thanks for its omission and Ulrika's response surprised me.

"Your father's heart attack turned him into a Democrat," she said.

"Huh?"

"Like former President Clinton after his heart attack. Both are now vegetarian."

The next morning's breakfast brought a bigger surprise.

Chapter 14

"You'll be having another sister or brother," Ulrika said quietly, as we sat alone.

I choked on a bite of pancake before managing to swallow it down.

"That *was* a surprise," she said.

"A pleasant one," I sputtered.

"I'm telling Vladimir this morning," Ulrika said.

That Ulrika told me her secret first signaled our closeness.

"How far along are you?" I asked.

"Second month."

"Vladimir will be ecstatic. It'll give him another twenty years," I said.

"He's had a hard life. Maybe it'll convince him to retire so you can take over."

Ulrika correctly interpreted my silence.

"You don't feel ready," she said.

"It's more," I said, with a sigh. "My kids are babies, Randy hasn't proposed, and most of the business is European which means that we'd have to live here," I said.

"You dislike Berlin?"

"No, I love it. But Randy is finishing his doctorate and doesn't take change well. Moving here would be a big one," I said.

"It won't happen soon. When I suggested retiring to Vladimir, he said it's healthier for him to work. Which may be seeing how obsessive he is." Ulrika said.

"There's too much going on. I can't get my head around that now," I said.

"You do seem troubled," Ulrika said.

"I don't feel certain what'll happen in Moscow," I confessed.

"It's good that you're nervous. Certainty leads to getting killed. Tell me about Page," Ulrika said.

"She deserves an obituary," I said.

Ulrika didn't bat an eye. Before retiring to live with Vladimir, she had been his most skillful operative.

Chapter 15

"Page never laughs. My therapist once told me that people without a sense of humor don't understand themselves and she's certainly confused.

"She's angry and frightened and hurting. Love is a mystery for her. She told me that when a teenager she loved a boy but what she really loves is money.

"She kept gold coins in an antique box in her bedroom. Saying how beautiful they were and fondling them before going to sleep. Another bedtime activity was studying her bank statements.

"Killing attracts her, maybe because it reduces her fear of helplessness and increases her wealth. But she doesn't kill idly, always profiting from it.

"'*She doesn't kill idly,*'" Ulrika repeated.

"Not when she feels safe though she quickly became antagonistic when believing that I'd made a move on her boss who was also her lover. Her eyes became like a snake's on *Animal Planet*," I said.

"That's something to keep in mind. She might be falling apart since until now she's been good at keeping her activities under the radar. But you'll be her friend," Ulrika said.

"She'll think I am but she's really her own friend," I said.

"You're entering an unknown situation," Ulrika said, with evident concern.

"You're not whistling Dixie," I said, in a humorless tone.

"Life is more interesting when you're unsure where you're going," Ulrika said, supportively.

"What about when you're not sure if you're coming back?" I asked.

"You're a talented agent and it won't be that. Solving a mystery has a rhythm like a plot in a novel. There are many possibilities until you see the line of the story and begin eliminating them. You'll sense when the climax approaches and know what to do."

I didn't reply. Ulrika's advice is always good and I had been gloomy enough for one day.

Chapter 16

Saying farewell in Berlin was more painful than in America since I didn't often see this side of my family. Beauty's clinging caused me to realize my importance in her life. She had had no contact with my children and I vowed to remedy this. Maybe, despite Randy's fear of change, we *could* live in Berlin, I thought.

The Aeroflot Business Class was like those of other airlines. It consisted of thirty seats spread across five rows in a two-two-two pattern. There was a personal television mounted to each seat and small footrests and storage places. I'm tall and had been advised to request a window seat where there is more foot room since it opens into the fuselage.

Underneath the seat controls on the center armrest were two power adapters. The television's remote control let one choose a program without using the entertainment screen. In a compartment were headphones and an amenity kit containing eyeshades, slipper socks, pen, toothpaste and a toothbrush, comb, lip balm, and body lotion.

Placed on my seat were a thick pillow, blanket, and a mattress sheet to provide a clean surface on which to sleep. Soon after settling in, I was offered water, wine, or orange juice and chose the juice.

I had never flown on Aeroflot and didn't know what to expect, having images of Communist era crudity in mind. But both male and female flight attendants wore sharp, perfectly garbed uniforms.

Soon came a welcoming speech by the captain followed by a safety announcement in Russian and English and the showing of a safety video, Menus were distributed just before the plane was cleared for takeoff.

Chapter 17

After liftoff, the pilot took twenty-five minutes before turning off the seatbelt sign which reflected the gloomy weather. Meanwhile I studied the menu and wondered what a *Mozzarella Ball Bococcini Mescium* salad was.

While taking my order, the flight attendant asked how I preferred to be addressed. Being an unmarried mother, this was a sensitive point with me. I smiled and told her "Margaret." Much bigger problems awaited me on the ground, I reminded myself.

Distribution of hot towels preceded canapes of cheese on toast on which I munched until the meal arrived. The service was better than on most airlines where a cart is rolled down the aisle. Here, a table was set at each seat with a tray being placed on a tablecloth. There were salt and pepper shakers and proper butter.

Being a semi-vegetarian, I rejected the appetizer of quail breast and smoked duck but ate the mozzarella cheese and dried tomato salad. I devoured the Chilean Seabass with rice and relieved my guilt at eating too many walnut-raisin rolls by rejecting the dessert offerings of chocolate mousse with strawberries or vanilla ice cream with chocolate shavings and mango sauce. However, I did eat the chocolate in Aeroflot packaging that came with the bottled water.

As the sun set, the weather gradually improved and the view throughout dinner was beautiful. Eating had a relaxing effect and, once the dishes were removed, I reclined my seat and had the usual absent mother worries. How often did my babies think about me? Frequently, I hoped. Did Randy, their father, *really* miss me? Of this I was less certain. I sighed while considering my full young life.

"Do you have friends in Moscow?" the man in the neighboring seat asked.

Chapter 18

I returned his smile and noted the cold blue eyes. From within the human survival instinct, my reptilian watchfulness sprang into life. Despite his friendliness, I didn't like him.

"Yes, I replied, briefly.

Ignoring my disinterested, he continued.

"Are you a student?" he asked.

I didn't want conversation and especially not with him but politeness won out.

"Yes, at Barnard," I fibbed.

This wasn't exactly a lie since I hadn't officially dropped out. After giving birth I took occasional classes online and had twice travelled into Manhattan to take in-person classes. I would earn my degree about when my children graduated elementary school if ever. But he needn't learn this. For my seatmate, I would be an ordinary college student as I practiced using a phony identity.

"What are you studying?" he asked, moving closer.

"I'm not sure. Maybe English, and then teach," I said.

"A worthy profession," he said.

His slimy manner disturbed me and I threw him an idiotic smile. I had learned that it sometimes pays to act dumb.

"I'm Harry, an accountant from New Jersey. Exploring Moscow while the wife buys out Paris," he said.

My dopey smile remained as I reached for the sleep mask from my kit.

"I'm tired," I said.

I turned away, put on the mask, and was soon asleep.

In the dream, the children were sleeping and Randy and I were alone.

"I've missed you!" he said, gruffly.

A touch on my thigh awoke me. Harry's breath stank of alcohol as he leaned over. Behaving instinctively, I reached for the TV remote to smash his nose. Before I could act, hands grasped his neck and pulled him away.

MARGARET IN MOSCOW

"I think we'd best change seats," the voice ordered.

Chapter 19

I felt enraged and wanted to kill. Harry had molested me: *a mother*! Though illogical, his action seemed worse than had I been single. This feeling remained even as my reptilian wariness faded and I looked up at the speaker.

He was about sixty. Tall and sturdily built, his hands had easily pulled Harry up. With liquor-glazed eyes, Harry sank into an empty seat two rows down. My rescuer slipped into the seat beside me.

I wanted to thank him but couldn't speak. "Breathe deeply and reboot," he said, in a kindly tone. I did and smiled, having often used the same phrase with my children.

"I couldn't help noticing," he said.

"Thank you. You stopped me from breaking his nose and making a scene. He was just a stupid drunk," I said.

He noted my replacing the TV remote in a bin and understood.

"*That* would have done it. Are you being met at the airport?" he asked.

"Yes, by my uncle," I said.

"Perhaps you should tell him."

"I think not. It would upset him and it's over."

"Do you want to inform the pilot?" he asked.

"No, it's over. But thank you again," I said.

I didn't feel like talking but felt obliged to. A knight who saved your honor deserves a reward even if it's just a few minutes of your attention.

"Have you been to Moscow before?" I asked.

"Many times, years ago," he said.

I suddenly became interested. He might be a Russia expert and I could use the knowledge.

"What brought you here?" I asked.

"I was the American military attaché assigned to the embassy," he said.

"Do you still work for the government?"

"No, I've just retired. This trip is for pleasure."

"I've heard that Russia has many attractions," I said.

My statement kept the conversation going yet revealed nothing about me.

"Yes, it does," he said, beaming.

His smile seemed too broad and, perhaps recognizing this, he explained.

"I've come to find the greatest love of my life," he said, in a tone that left no doubt.

Chapter 20

His twinkling eyes and statement changed my mood and aroused my curiosity. But I also sensed that he needed to talk and I had long been described as a sympathetic listener. It took just a small push.

"'Love of my life' is teenage talk and though you do look young..." I wheedled, with a smile.

"Maybe it takes a teenager to understand. My grown kids don't," he said.

I smiled at being described as a teenager, my body feeling to age rapidly from bearing twins. We exchanged names and Gerald began his tale.

"I met Valentina twenty-eight years ago in Moscow. She was officially a civil engineer but everyone thought she was a spy and she'd suspected the same of me. We were both wrong. She was what she said and so was I.

"It was the end of the Cold War. Russia's government had collapsed with the fall of communism and Harvard economists were consulting in Moscow. There wasn't love between our nations but the hostility was over.

MARGARET IN MOSCOW

"I'm retired from teaching military history at West Point and long divorced. Babysitting grandchildren didn't appeal and I looked for work. A foundation asked me to write a history of Finland's 1939 war with the Soviet Union, to signal its important strategic lessons. I immediately accepted since it included a paid trip to Moscow and chance to find Valentina," Gerald said.

"Do you know where she is now?" I asked.

"No. Her husband was an alcoholic brute and she feared our meeting. We'd met at her mother's apartment so I plan to begin there. This may be my last chance for love," Gerald said.

His eyes became tearful and mine did too.

Chapter 21

"Love will come in a way that surprises you," I thought aloud.

"*What*?" Gerald asked, with shock.

"Love will come in a way that surprises you," I repeated.

"I've just lost forty years. That's what I was thinking," Gerald said, with a smile.

A comfortable silence descended, the feeling that people get when they're on the same wavelength. I relaxed and looked out the window. The weather had changed into thick fog.

Flying switches you onto a global circuit, connecting you to foreign places even if you never actually go there. It gives a feeling of timelessness where it's never too early to nap or too late to eat. Lifting us from our usual rhythm and life through distance and disinterest. Flying had always seemed the start of an enjoyable exciting adventure.

This time felt different. Inexplicably, I thought of who I had chosen as my children's godparents if Randy and I were to die. I'm young. Why am I thinking this now? I asked myself.

"What brings you to Moscow?" Gerald asked.

His question broke my gloomy thoughts but presented a problem. I liked him and sensed, despite the age difference, that we could be friends. One shouldn't lie to friends so I told him a little of the truth.

"I'm visiting my uncle," I said.

"Have you seen him often?" Gerald asked.

"No," I said.

Then, realizing this wouldn't do, I *did* lie.

"I was adopted as a baby from a Russian orphanage. I recently found my uncle and this is a first visit," I said.

This fiction satisfied Gerald and impressed me.

"Love will come in a way that surprises you," he mused, with a smile.

We leaned back contentedly. I closed my eyes and vowed to sleep for the rest of the flight. Which I did until being awakened by a nightmare.

Chapter 22

I analyzed the nightmare. Not wondering why it occurred since frightening dreams, as my past therapist had told me, simply indicate your unconscious mind's insistence that *something* frightens you. Which was certainly true about my upcoming mission in Moscow.

Yet this dream contained an airplane crash and flying had never scared me for it meant being pampered and temporarily carefree. But to return to my dream.

I was calm at takeoff into the brilliantly blue sky. The flight would be brief. I would reach the beach resort with my boyfriend, Randy, the pilot, in just minutes. Then things began feeling strange.

Instead of a four-engine jet, I was flying in the small, misshapen box of a Cessna which floated and bobbled slightly as small planes do. I tried speaking to Randy but the whine of the single-propeller made conversation impossible.

The ocean sparkled as if littered with diamonds and I focused on it to reduce my growing panic. Soon came the welcome sight of a small landing strip in a green field surrounded by hills. Randy began the plane's descent and I waited for the thud as wheels stroked the pavement, indicating that we were on the ground and the start of our magical weekend.

But the plane was going too fast. It swooped past the runway as Randy fought with the controls to get back in the air. Emergency alarms unsettled me and Randy shouted into the radio, "MAYDAY. Downdraft and I can't get elevation!" The plane's nose tipped, heading toward trees as the sky disappeared.

Chapter 23

A wing clipped the treetops as the plane lurched into a dizzying ninety-degree swing. Branches lashed at the plane, tearing it apart until we slammed to a stop. The seat belt cut at my waist as the plane tried catapulting us out.

Everything went black so I don't know how long I was unconscious. When I came to feeling dazed, I looked at the wrecked interior and hugged myself, unable to believe that I was still alive. Relief slipped away and my heart pounded when I realized that I was squashed in the back of a crashed plane. Pain coursed through me and I nearly passed out. The plane's interior squeezed inward, sucking the air from my lungs.

I shouted at Randy, "Wake up. We have to get out!" He groaned and began moving, knowing that the plane could explode at any moment. We stumbled out into the darkening forest, fearfully dragging ourselves from the impending explosion with adrenaline overcoming pain.

Blood streaked our relieved faces as we collapsed onto the ground. Randy sat dully, in shock and unable to respond. I realized we needed to be found. Spending a night in the forest after barely surviving a crash would be too much. My breathing became ragged as I forced down my terror at this outcome.

Then I heard it. Embracing Randy, I screamed into his face, "Dear God, we're saved!" As the rescue helicopter approached, I felt a touch on my arm and burst awake.

Chapter 24

I instantly realized where I was and that the touch on my arm was Gerald's.

"You were whimpering, probably having a nightmare," he said, with concern.

"A bad one, a plane crash of all things," I said.

I breathed deeply to slow my racing heart.

"Do you want to talk about it?" he asked.

"Would you want to listen?" I replied, with a small smile.

"We have time," he said, sympathetically.

"It went like this. I'm flying in a small plane with the pilot who's my boyfriend. The plane goes down in a forest. Though injured, we'll soon be rescued by a helicopter," I said.

"You're telling yourself you're an optimist."

"Why do you say that?"

"While at West Point, I wrote a book about soldiers who suffer from Post-Traumatic Stress

Disorder. The mind can tolerate only limited stress. When exceeded, nightmares can develop. Almost all the veterans who I studied had them. Some woke up screaming several times a week."

"It's been like that with me," I revealed.

Gerald gave me a questioning look.

"I've led an unusual life," I said vaguely.

Revealing oneself to strangers, no matter how well-intentioned they seem, is never a good idea. Gerald didn't press for an explanation.

"Well, in my unprofessional interpretation of your dream, it sounds like you're telling yourself you're a survivor. I'd say that reflected an optimistic personality, wouldn't you?"

"Or a lucky one," I said, nodding.

"That luck may bless us both," he said, raising a bottle of water to his lips.

As I joined the toast, I noted that my breathing had returned to normal.

Chapter 25

"How long will you be in Russia?" Gerald asked.

"That depends on how many relatives are willing to meet me," I said, adding to my fictional narrative.

"I don't know why they wouldn't. They would be proud."

"Families can be strange. My existence may uncover secrets they prefer to keep buried," I said.

Before my tale became a romance novella, I changed the subject.

"What's the life of a college teacher like? We students view them as gods," I said.

"There's nothing godlike about it," Gerald said, with a laugh. "It's just the opposite since real power is had by administrators. I'm not the best one to ask, having earned my degree while in the military."

"Is that typical?"

"No. My career wasn't. I'm one of the few Army generals who didn't graduate from West Point. I enlisted as a high school dropout, becoming an officer without a college degree."

"You were commissioned without a degree?" I questioned.

This surprised me. Even I knew that a military officer without a college degree is so rare as to be nearly nonexistent. For Gerald to achieve this meant he must have done something exceptional, perhaps gained a battlefield promotion.

"I earned it later. One can't rise without a degree. I liked school but had to work at two jobs to help my family survive."

Upon learning this, I warmed to him. I had been poor as a child too but telling him wouldn't fit into my tale.

"Looking back, it's hard to believe my life. It's the greatness of America that people can realize their ability regardless of where they began," Gerald said.

"If they're lucky and prejudice doesn't hinder their way," I said.

"I'll agree with that," Gerald said.

Chapter 26

Gerald's hunger to tell his story kept from having to expand mine. And considering his kindness to me, listening was the least I should do. He seemed nervous, as would anyone whose happiness depended on make-believe. Was Valentina alive and, if so, was she married or would she barely remember him? What would he do then? A tragedy is when a fairy-tale love goes bad.

I easily thought of an alternative. Gerald was an educated, attractive, older man. Singles like him are prized by party hostesses who are eager to introduce him to their friends. But I sensed that wasn't how he viewed himself. In *his* mirror was an aging failure, a loser at love. Valentina was his last chance for happiness and no fact could change this belief. Love rarely responds to logic. Because childhood is the bedrock of personality, I wasn't surprised when Gerald's story began with that.

"I was born in Lithuania under Communist rule. When I was seven, my parents escaped to West Germany in a harrowing trip during which we had to walk part of the way. There, an uncle took us in and my father found work in a gym. He was a gymnast who'd competed in the Olympics. Six years later another relative sponsored us and we emigrated to America.

"Life in Texas wasn't easy. We barely spoke English so the only job that my father could get was as a school janitor. This and my limited English gave me a low status at school. The bullying stopped after I broke the nose of my biggest tormentor.

"But my family persisted. After learning English, my father got a job as a sports coach and I worked evenings in a gas station and weekends at a supermarket while attending school."

"You had a rough time," I said, sympathetically.

"Our lives would have been worse under Communism," Gerald said, with a small smile.

Chapter 27

Gerald's story got even better.

"Then I made a serious mistake though maybe not since fate creates its own path," he said, reflectively. "I'd saved enough money to get an old Camaro to drive to school. A friend noticed its missing hub cap and said that I could get one at the scrap yard for ten-dollars which I didn't have. He knew where these parts were stored and volunteered to steal it. It was risking much for little but we were drunk and not thinking clearly. We waited as he climbed over the fence. Moments later, a police car caught us.

"At the station house, the policeman said it would go easier if we told the truth. One of us fell apart and confessed. I told the judge I planned to enlist in the Army and that a conviction would end this possibility. Texas is a patriotic state and he bought my story, ordering a deputy to accompany me to the recruitment office the next morning.

"That was how it started. I advanced from infantry private to paratrooper to the Special Forces where my fluency in Russian and German was prized. While climbing the ranks, my education progressed from a college degree to the Army War College and Harvard."

"That's some life! You could write a book about it," I exclaimed.

"I've written several but none about me. I'm not vain enough to consider my life of interest to anyone but my kids. And maybe Valentina," he said, with hints of sadness and hope.

Chapter 28

A listener can't remain silent for at some point they must contribute to the conversation. Yet I was running out of fantasy and am a private person. Tell me your woes but I'll reserve mine is my creed. This doesn't hold when with my parents or sisters or best friends though sharing some matters with a boyfriend can cause problems.

"My life is simple though there is romance," I said.

"If not at your age..." Gerald said, supportively.

His look was sympathetic and my imaginary tale grew.

"Adam is also a student but unsure what he wants with me and everything. We'll graduate next year. Then I'll teach but he doesn't know what he'll do," I said.

"What's he majoring in?" Gerald asked.

"Geology."

"There're many things he could do. Work for an oil company or teach Earth Science in high school. What's his problem?" Gerald asked.

I added some truth since a lie is most believable when close to it.

"He's very smart but is...*confused*. He wants to be self-sufficient but isn't. We've dated since we were thirteen and I pretty much manage his life which he needs. He's always ignores his mother's demand to get a haircut but not mine. We've spoken of marriage but only tentatively, if it would be best or not. I've offered to support us until he figures out his life."

"That might not be a good idea," Gerald said.

"Why not?"

"People can resent those who they depend on even if their life requires it," he said.

"You're probably right," I said, nodding.

He was. Years before my therapist had told me the same.

Chapter 29

My tale had seemed realistic even to me so I felt no need to expand it. We shared enough and the comfortable silence between us grew. I gazed out the window before focusing on the Russian spoken by a Chinese passenger.

"You're surprised," he said.

"Yes."

"China was close with Russia before many Chinese Communists were slaughtered by Chiang Kaishek's Chinese Nationalists in 1927. Decades later, Chiang's son, who was originally a Communist, became Premier of Formosa."

"I never learned that in World History," I said, with fascination.

"I didn't know either until writing a book about it," Gerald said, humbly.

We both laughed and I was taken by how relaxed our relationship had become in mere hours.

"History books focus on politics but mine concerned day-to-day life. Like that of the Chinese students who came to the Soviet Union during its early days. Being a student, you may find it interesting."

"Yes," I instantly agreed, always enjoying hearing a scholar speak on his specialty.

"After being massacred by the Nationalists, the Chinese Communists sought military training to battle Chang Kaishek. For this they turned to the Soviet Union who considered China more favorable to Communist ideology than Europe.

"The early Chinese students who came to Russia were filled with romantic revolutionary ideas. Once there, military education dominated but this wasn't what many of them wanted. Some had plainly been kidnapped. Picked off China streets and ordered onto a boat, believing they would be studying at the renowned Sun Yat Sen University but becoming stuck at a military training camp. There, they faced bewildering emotional and cultural challenges and starkly different food and weather.

"Letters and petitions were sent to officials, begging to be transferred. A girl wrote, 'our bodies are not strong enough to be good soldiers.' A man refused to wear a uniform and burst into tears when he was denied a transfer from the military. Many were physically unfit and desperate to leave but not all. Chiang's massacre had convinced the Chinese Communists that to survive they need take up arms though some students preferred those of local girls who were supposedly tutoring them in Russian. Not very different from American college students were they?" Gerald asked rhetorically, with a smile.

Chapter 30

I tried keeping an interested expression as my eyelids drooped. Noting this, Gerald courteously said, "We're both worn out," leaned back and closed his eyes. The steward's arrival with the dinner menu awakened us.

Whether from anxiety or hunger, I didn't hold back. As appetizer, I had a pancake with salmon, cream cheese, and caviar. Salad was the usual greens, tomatoes, mango, and honey-lime dressing. Being a semi-vegetarian, I ignored the salad's duck breast and didn't order borsch (beet soup) since it contained beef. As main dish, I had the black cod with coconut-lime sauce.

Gerald ordered the stuffed chicken wings with barbecue sauce. He did order borsch remarking, "when in Russia." Borsch is a classic Russian dish, even more than America's hamburger.

We ate silently as nearby conversation flowed with food choice taking an over-the-top time for some. But the steward was unfailingly courteous and patient, even with what seemed inane questions like asking if the chicken had been free-range. Behavior at home is one thing but when traveling abroad you represent your nation so silliness counts.

Following an uneventful landing at Moscow's Domodedovo Airport, Gerald and I walked side by side to the passport control counter for foreigners. While my passport was checked, the immigration official filled out an immigration card with entry and exit dates. One remains with the official and the other you keep with your passport. The card is needed to register at a hotel and must be returned when leaving the country.

I was uncertain how to complete several questions. Because stating that my purpose was business would arouse unwanted attention, I wrote "tourist." For length of visit, I wrote "one month" and gave my uncle's name as "host person." Reading this, the official smiled nervously and, after conferring with a colleague, asked me to wait in a nearby room. Gerald had already completed the procedure and worriedly asked if anything was wrong.

"No. It's probably that my host said he would have a car sent for me," I said, with a smile.

I didn't want to reveal his family name. My uncle, Borya, is a highly ranked security official and hearing his name tends to make people nervous.

Chapter 31

Gerald insisted that I take his phone number and I gave him mine, it leading to an answering service in New York. I would remain anonymous in Russia.

I was conducted to a room containing a table and three chairs. It was furnished for interrogation and not comfort though the official asked if he could bring me coffee or tea which I refused. He assured me that my car would arrive soon and I began reading on my phone.

Before leaving America I had downloaded an old novel, *Time and Again*, for its plot resonated. In it, an American secret agent goes back in time to nineteenth-century Manhattan. There, bearing a false identity, he tries to understand a past event though this isn't his official mission.

While reading, I realized this was also what I hoped to do. My approved mission in Russia was to prevent a possible killing, resulting in the likely execution of the murderer, Page. I hoped to thwart this since we had once been close.

Three years before, while working undercover in Manhattan, I had collected enough evidence to convict Page and her boss of murder. He was subsequently killed but she, being beautiful and persuasive, avoided trial by fleeing to refuge in Russia. Talented assassins like Page are rare and quickly hired by governments.

As my double role had been kept secret and we had bonded, Page still considered me her buddy. Through our friendship, I hoped both to gain information and to save her life. Despite her wickedness, I liked her. During our weeks together she shared the teenage rape by her father which I considered the unconscious motive for her murderous feelings.

I experienced a painful childhood too and, with naïve sentimentality, viewed her as still innocent, envisioning her life as it might have been but regrettably wasn't.

Chapter 32

Life is more precious when you've survived a few bad scrapes. Working undercover requires a strength of purpose, a quick mind, and mental callousness. I had become comfortable with kidnapping and justified execution. Thanks to these, several families were made safe and the world a better place.

Would it be better if Page were dead? Maybe not since people can change and I had no contact with her in years. Nor had Borya ever mentioned her except to say that she expressed concern about me and was assured that my life was fine too.

Page never learned my real identity and certainly not that I was a mother. If unchanged, she wasn't a person to trust since she had been wicked, and clueless about her uncontrolled temperament and impatience with limits too.

Page had lived unthinkingly from day to day, not considering what she was doing. She had a persistent will to gain money, considering morality to be an abstraction which she lacked. Though outwardly caring, she was incapable of love. Happiness for her was the ratio between what she demanded and received.

Page's thinking had been shallow, judging value by cost. She lacked understanding that wealth couldn't replace what was absent from her life.

Page had been headstrong and brutal, always seeing the faults of others but none in herself. Never questioning the consequences of her actions but pressing on, heeding no one's voice and being morally blind.

Before leaving America, I had told this analysis of Page to Borya.

"You know her better than anyone. That knowledge might save her life," he said decisively.

But he didn't sound confident.

Chapter 33

Foreign travel had always excited me but this feeling receded while waiting. I would soon meet a woman with whom I once lived. We had joked and shared, though she with greater honesty and openness. With Page, I would be a stranger and not myself.

I could leave now, insist that one of my children were ill and be on the next flight home letting events take their course, Page would survive or not and none would criticize me. I rose with this intention before sitting back down as emotion overpowered sense and fate propelled me along. Feeling unsteady, I clutched the chair's arms. Reality tends to blur when a life is grounded in deception.

Who is Page really? I again asked myself. The lack of moral people to conduct assassination required hiring scum who kill for the joy of killing. Deluded by their violence into believing they were shrewd but being simple criminals with a dreadful need for blood.

Page's beauty devastated people, caused men to not know how to react. She considered her appearance a useful genetic fortune, never seeing herself as others did.

As if her appearance were something apart from what she considered her inner real self.

Her extreme good looks were wrongly interpreted. Men couldn't think beyond her surface, get beneath her appearance to where she really lived. She had told me that, when loving her, their face held a look of bliss and devotion.

Enough, I told myself, shaking my head to close this line of thought. Worry is a needless pastime. Over-thinking weakens concentration and would disrupt the single-mindedness I needed.

Borya once said that though he believes me to be lucky, it was a mistake to rely on it too much. "Luck can swing away and favor your enemy," he warned.

Chapter 34

The door was finally opened by a tall woman of about thirty-five. Her police uniform bore shoulder patches with three stars which she later told me ranked a Police Senior Lieutenant. Accompanying her was a male, two-striped Police Junior Sergeant.

They would provide my transportation, I was told. My luggage had already been retrieved and we walked to their Mercedes without speaking. Their car surprised me, I having expected it to be a Russian Lada or UAZ or Skoda though it didn't matter.

I was directed to sit in the rear seat with the lieutenant while the sergeant drove. Though feeling edgy, I dismissed the weird thought that I had been arrested. None would *dare* arrest Borya's niece, I told myself, and hoped this was true. Russia had a long history of imprisonment and execution with most being unwarranted. To distract myself from these gloomy thoughts, I studied the passersby as the car sped with flashing lights and blaring siren.

I wasn't told where we were going and thought it best not to ask. If I did, questions might follow and my ability for fantasy had been exhausted during the long plane ride. So I concentrated on the street scene.

The Russia scenes in old movies hadn't prepared me for what I saw. Not drab women washing sidewalks but proud figures dressed in bright colors or the West's collegiate style of dark hoodies, capes, and stylish scarves. And unlike in the United States where it has become taboo, long fur coats and large fur hats were common and favored by the older women.

A young girl holding her mother's hand wore an ankle length, hooded, yellow coat. Teenage boys, as you might expect, sported grungy black jeans and jeans jackets though their backpacks were colorful.

I couldn't help exclaiming at the sight of a young woman dressed in a short red jacket and short black skirt, thigh-length black boots and large sunglasses, as she confidently strode the street, her glossy black hair flowing in the wind.

"The women are so well dressed. It's like New York's Madison Avenue," I said, excitedly.

"It's the new Moscow," the lieutenant said proudly, with a smile.

Chapter 35

My anxiety disappeared as our car approached the Marriott Grand Hotel, its American brand reassuring me. I had been pre-registered and was quickly shown to my room.

"Your uncle is engaged but will arrive for dinner. He asks that you not leave the hotel," the police lieutenant ordered.

"All right," I said, compliantly.

As soon as the door closed behind her, I left my suitcases unopened and inspected the rooms which overlooked Tverskaya Street.

The windows were sound-proof and actually opened and the ceiling was high. The suite consisted of a bedroom, a living room, and a work area. The living room was furnished with two comfortable couches, a heavily cushioned oversized chair, and a dining table and chairs. The writing desk had an ergonomic chair and electrical outlet. There was a radio and two TVs, a DVD player, and wireless internet that worked well.

The bedroom held a comfortable king-size bed. Subdued shades of yellow and brown predominated except for the pale pink bathroom. I had forgotten to bring a robe and slippers but found these and a hairdryer in the closet beside the bathroom.

According to instructions on the desk, the suite included access to a two-level Executive Lounge which held complimentary newspapers, business services, and snacks and desserts throughout the day.

I hesitated to leave not knowing when my uncle would arrive. But after feeling claustrophobic which I self-diagnosed as anxiety, I felt that I had to. To avoid causing his worry and misbelief that the policewoman had mis-conveyed his instructions, I taped a note to the door with Scotch tape which had been conveniently left in the desk, stating that I was exploring the hotel and would be back in an hour. I also left this message with the concierge who promised to deliver it upon his arrival. "Instantly," she nervously assured me. Did her anxiety reflect professional courtesy or Borya's position? I wondered.

Chapter 36

While peeking into the hotel's impressively skylighted Grand Alexander dining room, I received a summons from the concierge. Cutting my tour short, I hurried to meet Borya who didn't look pleased.

"You were instructed to wait in your room," he said, sternly, as his two hefty bodyguards coldly scanned passersby.

"Yes, I'm sorry. I was feeling suffocated from being stuck in a plane and later," I said, apologetically.

In such situations, tears usually work for a woman but I knew they wouldn't with Borya. If he believed I was that kind of woman, I wouldn't be in Moscow.

"We'll eat in your room," Borya said.

"Okay," I said quickly, knowing that I had rebelled enough.

We marched to my room with one bodyguard leading and the other bringing up the rear. After seeing their hard expressions, guests waited for another elevator.

Borya's meal was traditional Russian: *shchi* (cabbage soup with potatoes, carrots, onions, and chicken); *beef stroganoff* (fried chopped meat and onion sautéed with sour cream; buckwheat; and a tomato/cucumber/onion/dill salad on the side. As beverage, he ordered *kisel* which is boiled berries with sugar. The berries are filtered out with starch added to thicken, making it like melted jelly and very tasty. That he didn't order vodka indicated the seriousness of our talk.

I ordered *ukha* (a fish soup with clear broth), salad, baked salmon (which I love), and milk. Feeling that I also deserved something sweet (regardless of its effect on my hips), I indulged with *blini* (wheat pancakes rolled with jam and chocolate syrup).

While eating, Borya spoke conversationally of Moscow happenings: the nation's bewilderment at Poland's snub of Russia at the recent World War II commemoration, and the "monkey business" of a Russian's arrest in Indonesia for trying to smuggle from that country a drugged orangutan, two geckos, and five lizards in his luggage.

After concluding this story with a smile, Borya instructed the bodyguards to wait outside the suite. When they left, he turned toward me.

MARGARET IN MOSCOW

"Now we must talk," he said, gravely.

Chapter 37

My phone rang and I looked at Borya. "Answer it. It may concern your children," he said.

"I've been invited to a wedding. What do you think about wearing a white dress?" came the anxious voice of my oldest sister, Melody.

Feeling annoyed since this certainly wasn't an emergency, I breathed deeply before responding.

"Are you there?" she asked.

"I'm thinking," I said, before whispering to Borya, "be off in a minute."

"I wouldn't wear a cupcake gown and veil but a floral print on white should be okay so long as your shoes and hat and everything else is a color," I said.

I spoke with greater certainty than I felt, wanting to get off the phone.

"You're a treasure! Have to go," Melody said, before abruptly hanging up.

"What to wear to a wedding," I told Borya, and shut off the phone.

He nodded and patiently began his lesson.

"Have you seen the old movie, *The Great Escape*?" he asked.

His question was so unexpected that "Huh" burst out before I caught myself.

"No."

Retrieving a DVD from his briefcase, he placed it on the table.

"Watch it. The sofa would be more comfortable," Borya said.

We rose and seated ourselves in the sofa's deep cushions.

"This year is the seventy-fifth anniversary of what became known as The Great Escape. Malnourished Allied prisoners-of-war spent nine months digging a tunnel to flee a Nazi prison camp. Only three of the seventy-six escapees reached safety. The others were recaptured and fifty were executed.

"Though filled with falsehood, the movie tells enduring truths. The prisoners could have sat out the war but felt it their duty to escape. Other prisoners helped as lookouts or tunnel diggers or dirt disposers or forgers of papers, and more.

"Though from many countries, they spoke a common language of duty and sacrifice. Nazism was one of the worst tyrannies in history but even as prisoners the men triumphed by finding a way to be human again. They showed what individuals working together can do and what we will do.

I nodded understanding.

"The greatest error in battle is inactivity, an unwillingness to take sensible risks. Don't assume that Page or her accomplices will behave in a particular way and do follow orders, even if in battle it is often the orders you disobey that make you famous. Don't become famous!" he warned, trying but failing to add a comical note to his severe tone.

Then he reached over, made a real smile, and hugged me.

Chapter 38

Borya left soon after, having no more to say until something happened. Page had disappeared and until she reappeared there was nothing for me to do. Her prior absences had lasted from two to seven days so I had time to occupy as freely as I could. I was now permitted to leave the hotel but only with the bodyguard he assigned. "Consider her your tour guide," Borya said.

I phoned my babies, which is how I still thought of them though they weren't newborn. I had stopped their breastfeeding months before, being delighted to end this chore. Though it was late and I felt uneasy about disturbing their bedtime routine, my need to feel that they missed me won out.

Both moaned at my absence. They were staying with their grandparents who spoiled them rotten and our live-in bodyguard who had long been their playmate. Did James and Donna *really* miss me? I wondered. Surely, since their tears sounded real.

The conversation with my parents went harder. Unlike children, the vow of extravagant presents upon my return wouldn't pacify them. They needed reassurance I was fine, well cared for, and would soon return. Our conversation ended with my feeble cheery words.

If not a non-drinking Mormon, I would have relaxed with the expensively branded alcohol in the room's small refrigerator. Instead, I took a hot shower and watched *The Great Escape*.

As Borya described, the movie was Hollywood reality in which nourished, well-groomed prisoners of war capered and snappy lines overflowed. Still, I grasped Borya's lesson from it: that, working together, people can succeed despite great odds. And another which he may not have intended: that it's never too early to start thinking about your own skin!

So I did, leaving an envelope for him. It was addressed, "To Be Opened After My Death," and contained two things: a note and a Peanuts Diamond Embrace ring engraved with the words, "HAPPINESS IS A WARM HUG." Randy, the father of my twins, had given me the ring in high school and I always wore it. It was as much of a commitment as he could tolerate, which condition I accepted though not happily. The note asked that I be buried wearing it.

The ring was impossible to wear on my mission and I knew Borya would understand. He knew that, for a soldier, survival is often a matter of chance.

MARGARET IN MOSCOW

I had been sent to Moscow to carry out a mission. It seemed too big for one person until I remembered an old-time story. When a Texas Mayor reported a riot and asked for reinforcements, *one* Texas Ranger was sent. When the Mayor asked where the others were, he was told, "One riot, one Ranger." Then, in Moscow, I was that Ranger.

Chapter 39

Alexandra ("Alex"), was a tall, lithe woman in her late twenties. Dressed in black jeans and shirt, black leather jacket and sensible shoes, she could pass for an American graduate student. But the outline of a pistol gave her away as did her short, extendable baton which could deliver a lethal blow.

Speaking excellent English, she introduced herself as being one of Borya's assistants. She had been assigned as my bodyguard while I was in Russia. I nodded, smiled, and invited her to join me for breakfast.

Though not a vegetarian like me, her orders of typical Russian dishes were fine for us both: porridge made of oatmeal; *syrniki*, which is a baked biscuit filled with cottage cheese; and *sharlotka*, which is basically apple cake. I wouldn't weigh myself until returning home.

"Have you been to Moscow before?" Alex asked.

"No."

"What would you like to see?"

"What do you suggest?"

MARGARET IN MOSCOW

"Popular tourist sites are Saint Basil's Cathedral, Red Square, the Kremlin, and Gorky Park," she suggested, in the enthusiastic tone of a tour guide.

"They sound fine. Why don't we begin with the closest," I said, already feeling tired.

"Do you speak Russian?" she asked.

"A little."

"If anyone asks, I'll introduce you as my American cousin. Smile but speak little and never allow yourself to be separated from me. None *should* know of your presence here but one can never be certain. If danger arises, place yourself in back of me."

"I saw your pistol. So if bullets fly, your job is to take them for me," I said.

"You're the valuable one," Alex said.

Neither of us smiled.

Chapter 40

Alex reached into her jacket for a tiny pistol. It was a two-shot Derringer, identical to its forebears in old-time Western movies.

"What's this?" I asked innocently, though knowing.

"A present from Borya, just in case. He issued your license."

"It's like the Derringer of old," I said, hefting it in my palm.

"With modern improvements: a hammer-block safety and better materials. A serrated pad operates the extractor on the left side, and the safety is operated by thumbing the hammer back a fraction of an inch and pushing the safety in from the left side. It's a small caliber .22 Magnum so you need be close to your target," Alex said.

"I prefer small caliber," I said.

"Borya said you're a gifted shot," Alex said, approvingly.

She handed me six cartridges which I placed in the pocket of my jeans.

"I was once appointed an auxiliary Deputy Sheriff in Texas," I added with a smile.

"But the gun is only for an emergency!" Alex cautioned.

"Of course."

Personal security is serious stuff. When this topic ended, the tension relaxed.

"You'll find Gorky Park soothing. It had been drab but was renovated and is now one of the most extravagant urban recreation centers in the world. A place to rest from the City's hullabaloo. That is the right word? *Hullabaloo*?"

"Absolutely correct!" I said.

Though knowing Alex for only minutes, I instinctively liked her and sensed she liked me, having that look in her eye of *OK, pal, you're a pal.* This was important. My being more than just her job increased my odds of surviving.

Chapter 41

Alex' car was a four-door compact, a Russian Lada Vesta. That she could drive a manual shift, unlike the automatic shift on nearly all American cars, impressed me and I told her.

"It wouldn't take you long to learn," she said, supportively.

"Do Russian cars have automatic shift?" I asked, naively.

"Of course!" Alex said, with a laugh. "You must think we're in the Stone Age. This car has every feature of Western autos: airbags, an anti-lock braking system with brake assist, electronic brakeforce distribution, electronic stability control, traction control system, and hill start assistant. It even has a full-size spare which American manufacturers have done away with."

I noted more: the car's cup holders; a USB power socket in the central armrest which also contained a heating control for the rear seats; a color Touch Screen displaying the image from the rear view camera; an FM/AM radio with USB and SD card capacity; and Bluetooth.

"I'm sorry. This car lacks only the armor plating of my wealthy friend's SUV," I said.

Though true, I had spoken facetiously but Alex took my comment seriously.

"If we considered things would be bad, you'd see some real equipment," she said.

Alex' demeanor returned to tour guide upon our arrival at Gorky Park.

"It's empty because it's early. Soon there'll be runners and bikers, groups of in-line skaters, parents pushing baby strollers, and children on scooters. There are a dozen restaurants, a café selling thirty-six types of tea, and concessions selling corn on the cob, ice cream, and balloons," she said.

"Hold the balloons," I said, with a smile.

Our stroll began.

Chapter 42

Gorky Park was more Disneyland than Manhattan's Central Park. There were gardens for strolling but also restaurants, dance platforms, an outdoor movie theater, and an arts center containing an exhibition hall and concert space.

There were basketball and tennis courts, Ping-Pong tables, places for skating, bicycle jumping, skateboarding, and obstacle-course running. Trucked-in sand enabled beach volleyball too. We passed a fitness instructor leading people in Zumba workout and Alex said proudly, "It used to be a place for criminals. Now look at it."

Gorky Park was far cleaner than Central Park. Here, I would feel comfortable having my children walk barefoot on the grass but not there.

A child wearing a red helmet, who couldn't have been more than five, raced up and down the ramps on in-line skates, twirling in the air. Five-minutes later we watched a young woman in a white wedding dress and pink stilettos join children on an old-fashioned carousel. After descending, she posed for snapshots with her groom. "Russian women love to pose for photos," Alex said.

She grasped my arm and we approached a young woman in a short dress preening for the camera. "My American cousin wants to know why you are taking pictures," Alex said. The woman looked startled before smiling and saying, "Isn't it obvious? It is because I am so pretty." After Alex translated, I smiled too and replied with a Russian phrase that I knew: *"Bol'shoye spasibo vam"* ("Thank you very much.").

"What do you think?" Alex asked, as we left the park.

"It's impressive, really enjoyable," I said.

"It wasn't always so during my life," she said.

This had been her first private fact. I needed to know more.

Chapter 43

When your existence depends on another person, you need to understand them. To know who they *really* are, *why* they chose their career, and especially their life. If being responsible for the lives of *their* children, they might be less concerned with *yours*. I was unsure how to begin until Alex made this easy by asking, "Did you really stop the bioterror attack on West Point by yourself?"

"Borya told you," I declared, and she nodded.

"He loves me and exaggerates. If not for the Russian ski troops who were competing locally, both I and West Point wouldn't have survived," I said.

"Vladimir is your father. He is a famous general," she went on.

"Yes."

"But you live in America."

"I was adopted as a newborn. My parentage is complicated."

That was putting it mildly. My biological mother had concurrent affairs with a Russian general and a British spy. A DNA test was never done so it is uncertain who my actual father is. Thankfully, both men value each other and get along well. I love both. Now I risked my questions.

"Were you a soldier before joining the SVR (*Sluzhba Vneshney Razvedki*, Russia's Foreign Intelligence Service)?" I asked.

"No, though coming from a military family. My training began at School 1101 in Moscow. We had military uniforms in the closet and our motto was 'Russia is our homeland. We will defend it.' The education was civilian with advanced classes in math and computer science and cryptography. After college I became a member of the 72nd Special Services Center which specializes in psychological warfare. When I tired of sitting at a desk, I sought re-assignment and was accepted by your uncle."

"You were safer behind a desk. Do you ever regret your decision?" I asked, this being my key question.

"Never! I chose to defend my homeland as you've done for America. This makes your safety my most important task."

I sensed Alex' dignity and her strong moral code. She had answered my concern.

Chapter 44

"What would you like to see next?" Alex asked.

"The Kremlin. I heard the word in high school. Is it a building?" I asked.

"*Is it a building?*" Alex repeated mockingly, before explaining with a smile.

Her attitude hadn't been unkind, as if knowing that Russia must seem alien to foreigners considering its unique script and walled-off history.

"The Kremlin Territory is a 15th century fortress containing Cathedral Square which holds five churches, the Patriarch Palace, the Armoury Museum, and the Great Kremlin Palace. The Kremlin Palace is used for Presidential receptions. One can visit as a tourist but we'd have to show your passport which wouldn't be a good idea. Maybe we can return before you leave Russia," Alex said.

Since she was the expert I merely nodded agreement.

"We can see the Moscow Kremlin Diamond Fund by simply buying a ticket. Its collection is similar to

Great Britain's Crown Jewels and the Imperial Crown Jewels of Iran."

"That would be great," I said.

The Diamond Fund Collection was in two small, velvet carpeted rooms on the ground floor of the Kremlin Armoury Chamber. It contained the one-hundred-ninety carat Orlov Diamond and a ninety-carat diamond with Arabic inscriptions. The major attraction was the Great Imperial Crown which contains five-thousand diamonds and was created for the coronation of Catherine the Great. While viewing it, Alex remarked, "Borya said you are her descendant."

"He told this to a German official who'd put me down. 'We're really descended from peasants.' Borya later told me," I said.

We both laughed.

Chapter 45

There had been a long line to enter the museum and I was tired by the time we saw everything. Noting this, Alex suggested that we tour the rest of the Kremlin another day and I instantly agreed. I could have asked this but, as happens, courtesy had won out over common sense. Though only twenty-three, pregnancy and the raising of twins had taken its toll.

When comfortably sprawled back in the hotel, our conversation naturally turned to love. Was Alex Borya's mistress? I wondered. I knew that he was married but no more. Russians are notoriously secretive about their families though that my father in Berlin, Vladimir, had both a family there and a wife in Russia, was widely known. The truth about Borya came soon.

"Borya told me you have twins. Are you married?" Alex asked.

"No," I said simply.

"Hmm..."

"That's exactly how I feel," I said, and we both laughed.

"Men!" Alex said.

"They're an international problem," I agreed.

Alex extended her long legs, put her arms about her neck, and readied herself for *the* conversation which knows no borders. Hers was more than ordinary girl-talk: they were the invaluable conclusions of a smart, experienced woman.

"Much that you hear about love is garbage. It can't be defined and you don't know what it'll be until it happens to you and then you may not spot it. At first, the person may just be someone who got under your skin a bit deeper than most, someone you wanted sex with and would leave whether you slept with them or not.

"That's until you recognize what love is: the unbearable loss when they've not there; suffering as much as joy; seeing who you really are; the change into something both more and less than you were. This awakening doesn't come quickly but only after much shock and pain, and looking it too.

"None of these would have happened if I hadn't met him. I was living a normal life until everything changed. After falling apart I discovered my shady side, a lawlessness which Borya recognized and channeled."

The question burst from me.

"Is Borya your lover?" I asked.

Alex gave me a look as if I were crazy.

"God, no! He's a devoted grandfather and practically lives in the office. His greatest love is his work," she said, with a laugh.

Chapter 46

"You may conclude that I hate my ex-boyfriend, Oleg, but I don't. That love is gone and I feel nothing for him. It's as if someone who I loved had died and I'd mourned and moved on with no emotional baggage.

"I tried to figure out the point where it went wrong but there wasn't one. It had been gradual, our change in opposite ways condemned the relationship. It was unavoidable and I couldn't have stopped it. After realizing this, I understood myself and that I was better off without him.

"Afterward when we met on the street and he invited me for lunch, it felt unreal to be with him. It was as if he weren't there and what I faced was an intimate stranger. I waited to become angry but didn't, feeling only the emotional shadow of what had once burned brightly.

"My rebirth didn't come immediately. I moped at home for weeks, telling my boss that I was sick. If Borya hadn't invited me to his office, I don't know what would have become of me. I was in a bad way, way bad.

"Borya told me that providing service to the state is an honor, that bravery and integrity are rewarded with a sound mind and clear conscience. He said he knew my background and that I would be resourceful and courageous with him.

"There are moments when one must choose to leap or stand by and let the chance pass. These instants shape a future. I leapt into my future and saved my life."

Chapter 47

Alex' continued musing about her ex revealed that she was not yet over him.

"Oleg was spiritually killed by the military. He was sweet until they changed him. After college, he trained as an officer and was sent to battle terrorists. He must have been good since he survived when many didn't. His letters were painful to read. I still carry one."

Alex translated and read from it.

"Things are as bad as can get. You carry everything you need: rations and ammunition and your automatic grenade launcher. The weight pulls on your body when you walk, your chest holding belts of grenades like in old movies.

"Besides this are the tent and hatchet and shovel and rifle and sleeping bag, making you feel there's no way you can move. Until you take a second step and more, thinking only of the next and dying but crawling on.

"We sleep unwashed where we drop at night, too tired to get up but doing so the next morning. We've become like the terrorists: half-crazed and hating everyone."

"But his military service was eventually over," I said.

"It was and it wasn't. After being demobilized, he returned to school but then volunteered to fight again though not knowing why. He felt drawn to return, that a large part of his life was back there. It was as if his body had returned from the war but not his soul, or it might have been the narcotic of war that he needed. Nine months later he was discharged again and it was over. But by then he'd become impulsive and cruel so our relationship was over too."

Chapter 48

To cheer Alex (or maybe myself), I told her about my children. What does *any* mother want to talk about? But it was also because thereafter I had to absent them from my mind. For Page, I would be the whore and cheerful buddy who introduced her to a healthier diet.

"What does being a mother feel like?" Alex asked.

I understood her curiosity. It was something that I didn't know until after giving birth.

"The best answer is what my mother said when I asked her. She told me that it's having both the best and worst feelings. That being a mother means the continuing fear that a trivial decision will cause your child harm. That it demands tolerating criticism if your child isn't achieving developmental goals on time and worry that a doctor's advice might be wrong.

"Being a mother means keeping your child from doing what they want to do when their father hasn't and having to fight him about that. It means being the target of your child's rage just before they calmly ask what's for dinner. But it also means being told you're the most wonderful mother in the world which seems to make up for the rest."

"All that would exhaust me," Alex said,

"There's that too."

A look of tranquility and wholeness came over Alex' face.

"Love doesn't last forever. Loathing does," she said.

"Yes, Hatred is deeper than love since it's a natural product of the nerves and we can't change them," I said.

"I've been living alone for so long that I don't seem to mind it. Maybe I'm naturally solitary."

"I don't believe that. You've been hurt. When our work is done, you must come to America and see my babies. They'll liven you and can always use another auntie," I said.

Alex didn't say "yes" or "no." Instead, she sighed and said, "You should nap. Your uncle invited us for a late dinner."

Chapter 49

Alex woke me two hours later.

"I was more worn out than I thought," I said, stretching.

"We leave in ten minutes," she said.

"Where are we eating?"

"At an apartment Borya sometimes uses in one of the Moscow Towers. It's more private," she said, explaining further after my enquiring look.

"The buildings used to be called the Stalin High-Rises. Moscow was ruined after World War II. Stalin wanted it to have the grandeur of a triumphant empire complete with skyscrapers.

"Seven fortress-like buildings were built of Russian Baroque design with stone exteriors. At night one almost expects a fleet of Batmobiles to exit. They were the tallest buildings in Europe, intended to symbolize the modern Soviet Union. Over decades they fell into disrepair and only one, the Kotelnicheskaya Embankment 15, was fully renovated. That's where we're going," Alex said.

MARGARET IN MOSCOW

Had we gone to a restaurant I would have changed clothes but hearing our destination, I didn't bother.

"It's a huge building and hard to get to, taking a quarter-hour to reach the subway station. Using a car is difficult since the building is on the spit of the Moscow river and Yauza and there are long traffic jams. His apartment is a floor-through with five bedrooms, four bathrooms, a kitchen and laundry room," Alex said, as we walked to her car.

"Don't all Russian apartments have a kitchen and laundry room," I asked, in surprise.

"Before the 1950s most citizens lived in overcrowded *kommunal'naia kvartira* (communal apartments) where families occupied their own rooms but shared kitchen and common spaces. Only later did they get privacy and the new existence known as *kommunisticheskii byt* (the Communist way of life).

"The mass housing campaign after Stalin's death was especially popular. It was something through which people could feel that Communism worked and their pain under him and during World War II had been worth it."

Chapter 50

With its thirteen-foot ceilings and gorgeous river views, Borya's apartment was definitely not intended for a low-level worker. While completing paperwork, he asked Alex to show me around, saying that I might have to stay there someday.

The apartment had red, white, and pale blue walls and Ikea-like generic furnishings. The gleaming white bathrooms had a light pink floor, marble-looking tiled walls, and a bathtub and two sinks. The bedrooms were small but comfortable with thick mattresses and abundant pillows.

The white-tiled kitchen had faux wood cabinets, a tan tiled floor, and a rectangular table. The hallways were narrow but the apartment was spotlessly clean and, all in all, very desirable.

Twenty minutes later, Borya's bodyguard found us. Food had been delivered and was set on a table in the living room. It was typical Russian fare with some modification for health-conscious me: *pyrizhky* (baked puff pastries filled with cheese), and baked salmon (one of my favorites). Borya and Alex had *pelmeni* (pastry dumplings filled with meat), and *solyanka* (a thick soup filled with sausage, bacon, and vegetables) with pickles on the side.

Borya's initial dark expression caused me think that something had gone wrong with my mission. But this didn't seem the case as his face brightened upon seeing us. He turned toward Alex.

"Has your mother closed on her apartment?" he asked.

"The seller hasn't gotten their Certificate of Sanity yet," Alex said.

"A person must *prove* their sanity to sell their apartment?" I blurted, and Borya smiled.

"Russia's commercial sector is new and pervaded by crime, as can occur in America too. In one scheme, a crooked sales agent plots with a property owner to sell their home before racing to a judge to cancel the sale because the seller was temporarily insane. The buyer loses their cash, the seller keeps their home, and they and the sales agent and corrupt judge pocket the money.

"Buyers can sue to reclaim their money but the laws routinely protect homeowners in these disputes which have numbered in the thousands. So to protect buyers, sellers must now show a Certificate of Sanity from a psychologist."

"Sounds weird but I guess it's logical," I said.

"Russia is very different from America," Borya said.

"I'm beginning to realize that," I said.

Chapter 51

While they drank tea and I drank milk, we schmoozed. Borya asked how we spent the day and I raved about Gorky Park and the Diamond Museum. Then I hesitantly asked the question which had been on my mind since leaving America.

"Am I part of a sting operation on Page?"

Alex looked at me sharply but Borya smiled benevolently as I acted the Dumb Valley Girl which I had perfected long before.

"I read an interesting piece online. A middle-aged businessman met two Russians selling military-grade weapons on the black market. They settled on a price of five million dollars and where the weapons were to be delivered, allegedly to be used by the Taliban to protect its drug labs against American forces.

"The businessman was persuasive. He said a down-payment of five-hundred-thousand dollars would shortly be wired and the discussion turned to ammunition and who would train the Taliban in the weapons' use. They snacked happily before separating. Upon leaving the hotel, the Russians were arrested and deported to the United States where they received long prison sentences. The article got me wondering. Are the suspicions about Page real or a sting meant to destroy her."

Borya listened thoughtfully. Alex looked uncomfortable and I understood why. His nickname of Lucifer (The Devil) hadn't been given casually. His orders weren't to be questioned but I was his niece. His answer came indirectly.

"Are you afraid?" he asked.

"Page is a killer. She'll analyze everything I say and do and I don't want a Columbian necktie," I said.

Borya understood but Page asked, "What's that?"

"What Colombian drug traffickers did to an undercover agent: his tongue was pulled through a slit in his throat," Borya said.

"It's *not* a sting," he said, looking at me steadily. "Page is rumored to be free-lancing and we're concerned. You're right to be afraid. Agents who aren't get themselves and others killed. But fear can exaggerate perils too, making them appear more dangerous than they are and leading to disaster."

Chapter 52

"OK. What should I do?" I asked.

I had been assertive enough. It was time for me to shut up.

Borya smiled, leaned over and touched my hand.

"Prepare for your role by ridding yourself of unneeded thoughts. Obsess over little things: the deodorant you will wear to conceal the smell of your fear, and the hair and clothing styles to better reflect your identity as a whore.

"Page loves money so wear expensive clothes and let the labels show. You are no longer *Margaret the Mother* but *Margaret the Escort*."

Despite my apparent serenity an unsettling feeling arose, like something left over from another life. I needed focus, not distraction. To gain control over my urges, I need eliminate feelings and the confusion they could produce. Worry disrupted attention and was an emotion I had no time for.

I knew that the only guarantor of survival is to eliminate the threat. Anyone can be killed if the killer has time and patience, is unconcerned with their survival and the target is unaware of their danger.

But I also believed what my therapist told me long before: that hope, courage, and willpower can achieve dreams. And survival too? I wondered, and smiled.

Borya had been watching me.

"*What*?" he asked.

"What I was once told: that hope, courage, and willpower can achieve dreams."

"There's much truth to that," Borya said.

"I do have one request," I said.

Borya nodded that he was listening.

"If I don't survive, my family is told they shouldn't be ashamed. That my death wasn't from being on the wrong side," I said.

"Both America and Russia will honor you. I will do all I can to assure your safety," Borya said.

"Okay then, *one riot, one Ranger*. It's what a Texas Ranger told a Mayor who called for reinforcements when his town rioted. When asked where the other Rangers were he was told, "One riot, one Ranger.""

"One riot, one Ranger," Borya repeated, with a broad smile.

Alex's comment lifted the mood.

"Tomorrow we'll shop for the clothes you'll need," she said.

Chapter 53

I never hope to be a fashion icon, buying most of my clothes in Greenwich's local department store, Richards. Erika, my best friend of a billionaire family, has other ideas. Long considering herself a "serious shopper," she travels to Manhattan weekly. There, Bergdorf Goodman is *her* store. I often accompanied her and became educated by her tastes.

Throughout most of my school years, until my family returned to prosperity after my father recovered from disabling Lyme disease, I dressed in hand-me-downs from my older sister and jeans and shirts from the Salvation Army store. Now I dress better, though fashionably only when it is essential. Mothers have more important things on their mind.

The next morning, Alex took me on a whirlwind tour of Moscow showrooms, from Chapurin Couture to the Arsenicum Showroom to the Denis Simachev establishment. When I asked the budget limit, she flashed a Eurocard and said there was none for my "whore outfits." Despite her accompanying smile, it took me a moment to realize the words were a joke. No woman, including a whore, wants to be called that.

The clothes she selected were definitely Russian: tight-fitting and colorful with flowing capes, high heels, and fur coats and hats. To accustom myself to this style, I changed in the store.

"These clothes should work. Men's eyes propositioned me all the way back to the hotel," I said later.

"Silly one, it's you, not the clothes. You're beautiful," Alex said.

"I've never thought that," I said.

"Why not?"

"I don't know. Even after succeeding at something, I tend not to credit myself. Maybe being an adoptee has something to do with it. The feeling that if my biological mother hadn't wanted me, I couldn't be much good."

"That's crazy," Alex said.

"Youthful beliefs linger and not all of them make sense," I said.

Chapter 54

Silences can draw people together when they know each other well. Other silences draw people apart when there is nothing more to say. While waiting, we talked politely about nothing.

We might have gone shopping or touring or simply walked the streets but weren't in the mood. Alex was bummed out over her lost love and my mind was on my children who, I hoped, were missing me as much as I missed them. It's time to find out, I told myself.

It was 10:30AM Moscow time which was 5:30PM Connecticut time. They would have eaten and been full of energy. Claudine, my youngest sister, answered my call and started in immediately.

"I'm going to Abigail's Period Party on Saturday," she said.

"That's nice," I said, without thinking, before adding, "Huh?"

"You know what *that* is, don't you?"

"Our mother embarrassed me with mine. I'll tell you someday," I said.

"Mine might be better. It's a confessional and mom wangled a doctor to give us advice as if we needed any."

"Closing the barn door after the horses are gone," I said.

"Right and mine is GOAT."

"Huh?"

"*Greatest Of All Time*! Don't you understand?" Claudine asked, with a hint of annoyance.

"I've gotten old. Let's hear it," I said.

"I was giving a talk in English when my first period came. I looked down, saw the stain on my white pants and heard murmurings. I calmly took off my jacket, tied it around my waist and continued my talk. You'd have been proud of me. I deserve an award for I don't know what."

I *was* impressed.

"You need quick to survive and you've got it," I said.

"Hundo P."

"Huh?"

"That means *one-hundred percent certain,*" Claudine interpreted.

Chapter 55

Claudine's banter and optimism raised my mood. So did James' and Donna's joy at seeing me even if only on a phone. They gushed about their trip to the playground and the ice cream which their grandmother permitted. I allow it only at birthday parties. Sweets are not food.

Finally feeling relaxed, I overslept that night. Upon awakening I was as serene and cheerful as one can be before sensing something menacing. A burdening thought which I couldn't quite remember but became clear minutes later. Disagreeable and vivid, it was like post-surgery pain when the opiate wears off.

What dagger hangs over me, I wondered? Why it's Page, of course. How stupid of me! When Alex arrived, she noticed the change.

"What's wrong?" she asked.

"My mission," I said, simply.

"What about it?"

"Honor and decency aren't suitable in all situations," I said.

"Yes, but this isn't an ordinary situation."

"No," I said.

"Look at it this way," Alex said. When Page freelances without government authority she acts as a terrorist. They're all emotional fuck-ups, unable to experience life with feelings unrelated to their immediate task. For them, people are mere fuses that burn out and can be replaced. And even when experiencing normal emotions, they don't know what to do with them.

"If Page is just swindling a billionaire, nothing will happen. Moncy makes her happy and Borya won't object. But if her actions effect national interests she must be stopped. Surely you see that. You're doing the Lord's work and that's how Borya sees it too," Alex said.

"I expect he does. I've noticed his tinge of grandiosity," I said, with a smile.

"What would you like to do today?" Alex asked, to avoid responding.

Since Borya was my uncle I could speak freely but he was her boss and, in this room, we couldn't be sure who listened.

Chapter 56

What did I want to do today? I asked myself, without receiving an answer. The obvious, which I couldn't, was to resume my normal life in America. I hedged.

"What do you suggest?"

"Further study."

"Huh?" I asked, using the childish verbalism which I hadn't yet outgrown.

"We study whores to get you in the mood," Alex said.

'You mean to *act* the role," I corrected.

"Certainly."

"How do you plan we do this?" I asked.

Three years earlier, when I played that role in Manhattan, I was tutored in the business by the escort agency's manager. I wondered what Alex had in mind.

"I've assembled two call-girls but don't want them seeing you. I'll question them while you watch and listen."

"OK. Where'll that be?" I asked.

"In one of our interview rooms. We'll go after breakfast," Alex said.

Breakfast was fried eggs for her, oatmeal porridge for me, and *syrniki* (cottage cheese filled biscuits) for us both.

"Dress casually," Alex instructed.

Our destination was Lubyanka. Built in 1898 as headquarters of the All-Russia Insurance Company, it is a yellow brick, Neo-Baroque structure and headquarters of Russia's Foreign Intelligence Service, the FSB. The old Soviet Union's hammer and sickle can still be seen on the building's façade.

After Alex' credentials were checked and a phone call made, we walked down corridors of beautiful parquet floor and pale green walls to the interview room. There, two beautiful, young women chatted, sipping drinks and at ease.

"It's worth their while to speak honestly: I promised each their freedom and sixty-thousand rubles," Alex said.

"Wow!"

"About a thousand dollars," Alex said, casually.

MARGARET IN MOSCOW

We sat outside the room. Watching through a one-way mirror as Alex interviewed them and interpreted.

Chapter 57

I soon realized that the women weren't young. Both in their thirties, they were slim with long lustrous hair and breasts that didn't need a push-up bra.

Alex' initial request was simple: "Tell me how you entered the trade."

Irina spoke first.

"None in my family know of my work. I was a low-paid programmer, looking for a decent, hard-working guy to marry but meeting only alcoholics. As I met people with other lifestyles, my idea of who I was changed. One of them suggested that I enter the occupation of 'escort' on an instant messaging profile. After a week of talking, I met a doctor at a hotel.

"The experience wasn't glitzy or even as sexy as I imagined but I later decided it wasn't that bad. With only one date a month I could pay for my car and have money left over. In the end, I gave up programming to work fully as an escort because I needed more free time. I was caring for my sick mother and the money was a huge benefit. You might say it saved her life."

"Do you feel bad doing your work?" Alex asked.

"Not so long as it's safe but the social and legal issues can affect my future and the people who know me and I love."

"What are your clients like?" Alex asked.

"They're generally doctors or engineers or executives. Most are married and attractive enough to get a mistress but they want a relationship without strings in order to keep their home life. Some are foreign students who don't know anyone."

"Do you know their real names?" Alex asked.

"I insist on knowing their full name and place of work, to contact them there before we meet. I check their identification through companies that work with escorts. Their database tells if a client gave women problems.

"What are your business expenses?" asked Alex.

"About fifty-thousand rubles (eight-hundred dollars) a month for my online ad and website, phone, and advertising. It's more if I'm traveling or there's a hotel expense."

"Do you regret being an escort?" Alex asked.

"I do and I don't. It's given me opportunities that I wouldn't have had but makes it nearly impossible to have a relationship so it's been a lonely life particularly after my mother died. I must hide my work from friends and relatives.

"The job takes its toll but I do think it should be legalized. Instead of wasting resources on arresting us, the state should give us opportunities and places to go for help. Women who don't want to be prostitutes shouldn't have to and those who want to should be able. But if it were legalized, I would probably have to lower my rates since more women would take up the work despite its stigma."

"Did your training as a programmer help you in any way?" Alex asked.

"I never thought of that though maybe it did. I'm better organized than the other escorts I've met."

Chapter 58

Though interesting, Irina's story wasn't new. I had heard the same about American call girls during a tutoring before a past mission. The next woman's information *was* new.

Alex asked Alena the same opening question: how she came to enter the business.

"Did you see the movie, *Tochka* (Point)," Alena asked.

"No."

"*Tochka* is a code word for Moscow's outdoor prostitute market on Tverskaya (Moscow's main avenue)."

"Yes, I know," Alex said.

Alena nodded toward the glass, as if to say that her explanation was intended for the observer. The women had been told I was an American sociologist.

"I saw it three times for it tells the story of my life. My parents were alcoholic. My father abused me and I left home at sixteen after giving birth to his child who I left with my grandmother to raise. I stole money from him to flee to Moscow. When the money ran out, I had only my body to sell. At least it'll be voluntary this time, I thought.

"The *Tochkas* are controlled by gangs who I avoid by staying off the streets. Irina and I share expenses. My boyfriend is ex-military and protects us. He won't let us wind up like happened in Nizhny Tagil. He is a good man and won't take money from me. I buy him things out of love."

"Tell the American what happened in Nizhny Tagil?" Alex ordered.

"A gang of pimps kidnapped women and forced them to work as prostitutes in their brothel. Those who refused were killed. Thirty bodies were found."

Alena gave a pleading look and I felt ashamed, both for her forced presence and her life. So apparently did Alex who immediately ended the interviews. She gave them their payment, a perfunctory warning to be law-abiding, and their freedom.

After escorting them from the building, Alex returned to the interview room.

"I'll suggest that Borya hire them for intelligence duties. This will protect them from the police and thugs," she said.

Chapter 59

Minutes later, we were summoned to Borya's office. Flanking it were frantically busy assistants and an armed guard who smiled and waved at Alex. One assistant nodded toward us and we entered Borya's office after knocking. Its appearance surprised me.

Instead of the modernistic design outside, his office reflected the nineteenth century. The ceiling was of exposed wood beams and the desk, credenza, and chairs were antique French. Light came from large curtained windows, a ceiling globe fixture, and old-fashioned table lamps.

But for the file cabinets, the room would appear a drawing room. Surprisingly, it contained no technology except for three desk telephones.

Borya greeted us with a big smile. He kissed me on the forehead and hugged Alex. Like some politicians, Borya is a hugger.

"How did your interviews go?" he asked.

"I didn't learn anything new about prostitution except for how things are here," I said.

"Good. Their femaleness makes women better spies than men. To paraphrase what Napoleon said about war: in prostitution, the amateur is often better than the professional."

"I hope it doesn't come to that," I said, in a mock severe tone before smiling.

Borya's smile indicated understanding and he nodded toward two sofas where we seated ourselves.

"Page has returned to Moscow. It's time you met her," he said.

I tried keeping calm though feeling that my heart had just skipped a beat. To give myself time to think, I made a neutral comment.

"Your office has good intelligence," I said.

"A nation can't know how good their intelligence is until it fails," Borya said.

I nodded agreement. His statecraft was widely acknowledged.

"Have you considered how you two might meet?" he asked.

This was important. Page wasn't stupid and to turn up at her door would arouse deep suspicion, just as if we met supposedly by chance in a store. I thought of a possibility.

"Introduce me as an SVR agent who has been hired to honey-trap an American diplomat. That'll make us pals again." I said.

Chapter 60

Honey-trapping is using a romantic relationship to take photos for blackmail or as evidence for a legal case. It is widely used in espionage to pressure an individual's cooperation and was depicted in several *James Bond* movies.

Mine was a good idea and Borya beamed.

"Haven't I always said you are a natural?" Borya asked, rhetorically.

I smiled though feeling that there were other qualities for which I'd rather to be recognized.

"You'll meet here, supposedly for a mission in which her help may be needed. But we'll need a target. I can't be sure who she knows and to bring someone in from elsewhere would take time," Borya said.

"Is this mission critical for American security too?" I asked.

"I would expect that. Page recently traveled to Washington and we don't know why," Borya said.

"Have you informed the CIA?" I asked.

The two intelligence services communicate informally when national interests coincide.

"No. We have nothing to say and her trip may have been innocent. Why burn a good agent?"

Those are good points, I thought.

Silence descended until I offered another idea.

"Someone I met would probably agree to act as target if he's sure it's in America's interest and you meet his price," I said.

"Do I not insist that the blood of Catherine the Great flows in her veins?" Borya said, with a grin.

"Please!" I said, unable to stifle a laugh.

Alex smiled but said nothing. I had told her earlier that Borya loves me and exaggerates.

"Who is this man and why would he help?" Borya asked.

As I described, his satisfaction grew.

Chapter 61

"I met Gerald on the plane. He's come to Moscow to find his lost, greatest love," I said.

Borya and Alex remained silent. This captured their attention as it should, being the storyline of countless novels. I continued.

"He stopped me from making a scene by breaking the nose of a bothersome drunk. I told him a fairy tale of why I was traveling to Moscow and he shared his life story.

"He was born in Lithuania under Communist rule. His parents escaped to West Germany and his family emigrated to America six years later. He learned English in high school and enlisted in the Army, rising to the rank of general. He speaks Russian and German, served as military attaché in Moscow, wrote several books, and taught military history at West Point.

"An unusual man," Borya said, slowly.

"Decent too. Twenty-eight years ago, he met Valentina. She was an engineer and each initially believed the other to be a spy but both were as they said. She was married to an alcoholic brute and they met secretly at her mother's apartment in Moscow. Gerald is now divorced. He's come to find her and see if there's hope for the greatest love he'd ever known," I said.

Borya thought silently when I finished speaking and Alex had tears in her eyes. I had sold my plan.

Chapter 62

"Can you contact Gerald?" Borya asked.

"Yes."

"Would he cooperate?"

"If it would be in America's interest and you met his price."

"Which is?"

"To find Valentina," I said.

"What if she's dead or unavailable?" Borya asked.

"Gerald is sensible and honorable. If convinced that you'd done your best, he'll do his," I said.

Borya thought for several moments. Then, turning to Alex, he asked, "What do you think?"

"It's a good plan. Page won't know Gerald. He speaks Russian and knows covert operations. I don't see how we could do better."

"Nor do I," Borya said, and turned toward me.

"You've been outside the Dark World for years so I've asked Alex to give you a refresher. It won't be anything new and may not be needed but I'll feel more comfortable. As I told you in America, I wouldn't have chosen you but there is no one else."

I readily agreed to Borya's suggestion. Only a fool would refuse what could better their odds of survival.

Alex' lesson began as soon as we returned to the hotel. While I relaxed on the chaise lounge, she sat opposite holding notes.

"Having Vladimir as father and Borya as uncle, I could probably learn from you, but..." she said courteously.

"You're following orders," I said, with a smile.

Alex nodded and returned my smile.

"In your new life, you must always vary your route for following a set routine will get you killed. While in the Dark World you must be unpredictable, strip away the conventions of your past life and fade into the background.

"You must be paranoid, always looking around corners and watching your back while memorizing the cars behind you. Awareness is critical to staying alive, pay attention to every new noise and notice anything out of the ordinary. But discreetly, to not reveal that you're clearing the area.

"If not on a seduction, wear sturdy, lace-up shoes. Loafers won't do if you must kick and they may fly off in hand-to-hand combat.

"Your past life is over so,, every night before you sleep, repeat to yourself that you're a call girl, not a mother," Alex concluded.

"A killer too," I said, soberly.

"It may come to that. One more thing: Moscow has become chaotic and dangerous. Some areas are virtually lawless, a playground for criminals and spies. Consider the entire city a Dark World sandbox where everyone plays without rules. Only the exceptional thrive in such places and you may be one of them." Alex said.

She ended her lecture with a smile which I was unable to return. Having a good imagination is not always an asset.

Chapter 63

Though feeling sure what came next, I asked rhetorically, "What do I do now?"

"Now you meet the other starring actor," Alex said.

"OK, but not at Borya's office. We probably shouldn't have gone there," I said.

"Those who saw you were trusted and with your wraparounds and stick-on mole you couldn't be identified. But I agree that you should meet Gerald elsewhere. This hotel would be safe."

"He'll want assurance that what we're doing is in America's interest," I said.

"That's being arranged with the Counterterrorism Division of America's Diplomatic Security Service. Gerald will be given a letter from the Secretary of State requesting his cooperation," Alex said.

Feeling flummoxed, I blurted what I was thinking.

"For that level of power, this matter must be critical," I said.

"Fear is high," Alex said, nodding.

I phoned Gerald who picked up on the second ring.

"Gerald, it's Margaret from the plane. Are I interrupting something?" I asked.

"Not at all. I was drinking coffee and wondering how to search for Valentina," Gerald said.

"I can help you with that," I said, firmly.

"How?"

"A Russian official will help if I ask," I said.

"You know someone *that* important?" Gerald asked.

"Yes. What I told you about myself wasn't all true," I said.

"That doesn't surprise me. Throughout my career, most things weren't exactly as they seemed."

Chapter 64

Gerald readily accepted my invitation to a late breakfast in my suite. I ordered for the food to arrive earlier, not wanting the waiter to see him. My appearance was current Russian style: high heels, short skirt, and lots of makeup. A rehearsal for my role as whore.

The food was traditional Russian: porridge, *grenki* (French Toast made with baguettes), and *vareniki* (dumplings served with jams and honey). Along with fruit, coffee, tea, and water.

When Gerald arrived, I introduced him around.

"This is Alex, my friend," I said.

When she rose, her jacket revealed the butt of her gun.

"Who packs a pistol," Gerald observed,

"She's also my bodyguard. And this is Andrew Mason who represents the Counterterrorism Division of America's Diplomatic Security Service. I'll explain while we eat," I said, suavely.

I waited until coffee was poured before continuing.

"Only part that I told you was untrue. I *was* a student but dropped out of Barnard after giving birth to twins and *am* an adoptee. My father is a former Russian general who now heads a private security company in Berlin. His partners are retired from the Central Intelligence Agency and the British Secret Service. My uncle is an official of Russia's Foreign Intelligence service, the SVR. I've been involved in operations since I was fourteen."

Gerald stared and I stopped speaking to let my revelations sink in.

"You're a most unusual person," Gerald said.

"No more than you. My toddlers call me mean," I said with a smile, using humor to lighten the mood. Before I could continue, Andrew interrupted.

"General, four years ago, Margaret helped foil a bioterror attack on West Point," he said.

Now Gerald *really* stared.

Chapter 65

I blushed, being praised causing this.

Turning toward me, Gerald changed the subject.

"How can you help me?" he asked.

"By finding Valentina. My uncle promises to do all in his power to find her. If alive, he will protect her. If poor or in ill health, she will be assisted," I said.

"What must I do in return?" Gerald asked.

"Nothing big though there is risk. I would be lying if I said there were none. You would pretend to be an American diplomat. Your name and biography will be added to the Embassy staff listing. I would be your honeytrap whore. I must rekindle my friendship with a call girl in Moscow and you'd be my co-star." I said.

"I would be a Russian spy and Andrew's presence indicates American approval?" Gerald asked.

"Absolutely! Margaret's target is an assassin who just returned to Moscow from America. Both governments want to learn what she's up to. She is *very* dangerous," Andrew said.

"Why not dispose of her?" Gerald asked.

"Because her lover is powerful. The President wants to avoid this unless it is crucial," Alex said.

"That's Russia," Gerald said, casually.

"It's no different in other countries," Alex said, with a tinge of annoyance.

"Touché," Gerald said, with an accepting smile.

Noting the warmth of his smile, the unexpected thought entered my mind that Gerald would be a desirable boyfriend. Before reminding myself I had a fiancée, that is.

Chapter 66

"You've made an attractive offer. What are the downsides?" Gerald asked.

The others said nothing so I took up the challenge.

"The downsides are the same for both of us. We don't know what Page is involved with nor what might happen. It may be a cakewalk but if she sees through me she sees through you. I've been lucky in my life but as I've been told, 'It's good to be lucky but one shouldn't rely on it too often.'"

The others sat stony-faced but Gerald laughed approvingly and I continued.

"Your part is the bit role, for occasions when I'll need a social escort. Then, we'll watch out for each other. We'll be meeting hard people," I said.

"I've met my share," Gerald said.

"My job is solely to gain information. Anything else will be done by others," I said.

"But we'll be out-and-about on our own," Gerald said.

"Yes. You could pretend to be a hustler, not quite honest. Bitch about your small salary and unappreciative boss. Give the impression that you're on the make and open to offers, legitimate and otherwise. This would improve my cover," I said.

Facing Gerald, Alex asked, "Do you want a pistol?"

"Russia isn't America. They're tough on carrying guns here," Gerald said.

"You needn't worry about that but try not to shoot anyone needlessly. Margaret is armed," she said.

With that, Alex removed a small pistol identical to the one that I had been given earlier.

Gerald's smile returned as he hefted it in his large palm.

"This makes me feel I'm back in the army," he said.

Andrew handed him a stiff white envelope.

"You are. By authority of the President of the United States you've been recalled to active duty for the duration," he said, in an authoritative tone.

"I've been drafted," Gerald said, resignedly.

MARGARET IN MOSCOW

"Nonsense! As they say in the military, 'You've volunteered,'" Andrew said, with a small smile.

Chapter 67

"I've missed it," Gerald said, in a compliant tone, as tension settled over the room.

Wanting to reduce the tension, I asked, "What about military life do you miss?"

After several moments of thinking, Gerald explained, with a pensive look.

"Little things, big things, even the annoyances. Mostly the structured life, I guess. The comradeship and extended family where all kids become everyone's kids. My wife kept snacks for the kids who wandered in and whenever you needed a babysitter there was always a neighbor to volunteer.

"Military life has its own culture and standards and language abbreviations. Soldiers answer to a higher calling: the elected President and God. Leaders are cherished and served humbly, with spouses silently doing what's needed wherever the family need go.

"Even the little differences are big. Wives are on the playground or phone during the day but evenings and pre-deployment are family time and you don't interrupt unless it's an out-and-out emergency. Military wives provide stability in their family though remaining strong can be difficult during times of combat.

"But there are annoyances too, just like in civilian life. Destructive gossip can destroy a career and frequent moves are a strain with some places having terrible weather. And the rank system, which is essential to military structure, doesn't work well for kids. Socializing among ranks isn't possible since it hinders respectful obedience on the job where life and death decisions are made.

"Still, the biggest complaint seems the long commissary lines. On payday, it can feel like the entire post is there with battling kids and each family's *two* shopping carts," Gerald concluded.

"You loved the military," I said softly.

"*I did, I did*," Gerald said, with a grin.

Andrew extended his hand.

"Welcome back, general," he said, with a broad smile.

Chapter 68

Andrew rose from his chair.

"My job is over," he said.

Hands were shaken and he slipped from the room, leaving us to chat over food. It felt good to be among friends, even new ones.

Naturally enough, I spoke about my twins who were on my mind. My presence was crucial in their life no matter how devoted the grandparents with whom they stayed. Alex and Gerald listened politely but I quickly realized that I was babbling.

"I'm sorry. Being afraid can make you talk too much and say dumb things," I said.

"You're not talking dumb and I wouldn't want to work with someone who denied fear," Gerald said.

"Lies and betrayal come to experienced agents easily," Alex said.

"That's true and I've done it before but this game hasn't begun. It wouldn't be good to be caught in someone else's game," I said.

"Life doesn't consult us for when consequential moments occur," Gerald said.

I smiled and said nothing.

"Moscow Rules," he said.

"What's that?" I asked.

"Old-time shorthand for how intelligence agents behaved to stay safe. Though since we have Russia's blessing, most won't apply to us. We needn't worry that the government will follow our car or bug our rooms. If Page's accomplices do, we're in trouble and it's time to get out."

"It's starting to feel like high school where joy was followed by disaster," I said.

"We'll pray for the former," Alex said, as her phone rang.

Her somber look ended our chatter.

"Page has surfaced, accompanied by an American," Alex said.

Chapter 69

There are moments when time seems to stand still and this was one of them. My parents told me they felt this upon learning of President Kennedy's assassination and, nearly forty years later, of the attack on New York's World Trade Center. I wasn't born during the first crisis and was a toddler at the second but it must have felt like this then: the sense that huge, unseen happenings were in play to sweep the world along.

"We're at war," Gerald said, somberly.

None of us tried to distort reality with positive words.

"We'll begin looking for Valentina," Alex promised.

"That's for later. Love softens the survival instinct," Gerald said.

"I know how to bond with Page," I said hesitantly.

Out of the blue, a perfect idea had occurred to me. But one so awful that I hesitated to reveal it and Alex noticed.

"*What?*" she asked.

"My honeytrapped lover wants to marry me, making him ripe for murder for his life insurance money," I said, barely able to contain a grin.

Both stared as if believing that I'd gone mad before their awareness steadied.

"That's *brilliant!*" Alex exclaimed.

"Provided that it's not too realistic," Gerald agreed, grinning.

I touched his hand before embarrassing us both.

"I'll love you to death," I said, in mock seriousness.

"That's *one* proposition I could do without," Gerald said.

I didn't reply. My blush said it all.

"It's part of a good plan. Another is how you've learned Page's address," Alex said.

"Through Russian intelligence. They want Page and I to team on some scheme. They're paying for her apartment so it would be natural for us to live together and what better place for Gerald's murder than in dangerous Moscow?"

Both looked at me piercingly, as if not quite liking what they saw: a ravenous tiger who had been freed from its cage.

"Your uncle wasn't lying when he said you're Catherine the Great's descendant," Alex said, slowly.

"*What's that*?" Gerald asked, with surprise.

"My uncle loves me and exaggerates," I said.

It wasn't the first time I said this and I suspected that it wouldn't be the last.

Chapter 70

I was so inspired by my brainstorm that I didn't realize its obvious flaw until Gerald pointed it out.

"How can you be both my honeytrapped-lover/soon-to-be-wife and live with Page as her chum?" he asked.

Alex came up with a solution.

"Gerald becomes sick and is hospitalized. You live with Page during his treatment," she suggested.

"That'll work. Page and I could even visit him in the hospital," I said, after several moments of thinking.

"It *would*. We'll do it!" Gerald ordered, in a commanding tone.

"Yes dear," I said, in a wifely manner.

This brought chuckles and more silent reflection.

"Arrangements must be made: finding a complicit doctor and hospital. Essentially, writing the screen play for our creation," I said.

"We're making an *Argo*," Gerald said.

MARGARET IN MOSCOW

"What's *Argo*?" Alex asked.

"A hit movie about the CIA's effort to free American hostages in 1979. To sneak them out of Iran, agents disguised as a film crew went there and left with the hostages disguised as actors for a phony sci-fi film called *Argo*," Gerald said.

"Was anyone hurt?" I asked, thoughts of my children becoming motherless re-entering my mind.

"No, it was completely successful. Even diehard Hollywood liberals collaborated and without payment," Gerald said.

"It will be the same here. You will have total government cooperation and need only call me if a problem arises," Alex insisted.

Silence again descended over the room and Gerald read my thoughts.

"It'll turn out well. I would like to meet your children," Gerald said, supportively.

"I'd want that too but for now a promise: that if I'm killed, you'll help guide their lives. I'd want them to be like you," I said.

Gerald nodded and grasped my hand. That moment, I couldn't hold back the tears.

Chapter 71

It became a matter of waiting since nothing could be done until the arrangements were made. Meanwhile, Alex and I mused about the unusual paths that our lives had taken.

"Maybe, given your origin, you could have had no other," she said.

"Possibly but each is a product of their childhood and apart from poverty when my adoptive father couldn't work, mine was ordinary. I'll figure it out someday," I said, casually.

Her phone rang and, after hanging up, she said, "Your uncle is on his way."

I primped a bit and waited. Twenty minutes later, Borya entered the room trailed by two bodyguards. In government service, the number of bodyguards indicates one's importance. After hugging me and nodding to Alex, he ordered she and the bodyguards to remain in this room while we spoke in my bedroom. Borya can be jolly but I sensed his gravity. He loomed over me as I sat, his voice slow and deliberate.

"As I've told you, if there were anyone else I wouldn't have involved you. That you agreed despite having young children shows your courage."

Why is Borya buttering me up? I wondered, as he continued.

"I won't give you a pep talk, as Americans say, but there are rules to keep in mind. Spying is a matter of watching and waiting, of appearing so uninterested as to become unnoticed like a fly on the wall. It's a mistake to seek information openly.

"Spying produces a desperate strain. A spy can tell only so many lies before burning out and becoming careless. Being suspicious is good but paranoia can cause you to hastily end your mission and accomplish nothing.

"If Page becomes suspicious, you must increase her trust by making your scheme to murder Gerald more real. If what we fear is in play, critical national interests are involved and she must be stopped at any cost. Do you understand what I'm saying?"

"Yes. That in the scheme of things, mine and Gerald's lives are unimportant." I said, after some hesitation.

MARGARET IN MOSCOW

"No, I'm speaking of *Gerald's* life. If you must kill him to convince Page of your sincerity, you must do it," Borya said.

At that moment I completely understood why Borya had been nicknamed *Lucifer* (The Devil).

Chapter 72

It can take a long time to really know someone and I hadn't known Gerald long. Yet I felt sure of my conclusion: that he was genuine, modest, and decent.

Many men could be your boyfriend but you would want only one type of man to marry and spend the rest of your life with. Gerald was him and I found it hard to accept having to kill him even if two nations approved.

Borya sat on the sofa and motioned me to sit beside him. There, he held me close.

"*Sladkiy iskrenniy* (sweet sincere one), I've shocked you," he said softly.

"No. You made perfect sense but Gerald is a good man," I said.

"Good men die cherished in war and to prevent them," Borya said.

Being unable to argue with that logic, I said nothing.

"It likely won't come to that. Meet Page's suspicions early by answering questions that haven't yet been asked. And I'm not ordering that Gerald *must be* killed. A good rule of running agents is to never commit to a final act. When a person says that something must be done, I know they're considering something mindless."

Though listening closely, I felt myself drifting inside a dream with events grasped through the misshapen reflections of trick mirrors and frosty glass. Would I now be given a book entitled, *Murder For Dummies*? I asked myself. This comical thought didn't seem humorous.

I suddenly realized how complex Borya was. Like Vladimir, my Russian father, Borya could be daring or careful, relaxed or stately, forbidding or caring, intolerant or patient, sophisticated or almost rural, rash or dallying, unscrupulous or moralistic. What inner rules govern which of these traits appear when? I wondered.

Such questioning is pointless, I told myself. When you've know someone for years, not everything need be talked about since fate can play a starring role. His killing order would never have happened if Gerald hadn't come to my aid on the plane.

"You must be a worse person than your enemy to win," I said.

MARGARET IN MOSCOW

"That's true," Borya said, with a smile.

"It should be. It's what you once told me," I said.

Borya's smile broadened but he said nothing.

Chapter 73

"Anyone can kill if they or their family's life is in danger but killing a non-threatening person is harder. Could you do it?" Borya asked.

"If it means getting home to my babies I could," I said.

Borya pulled back, possibly feeling that he had pressured me enough for one day.

"As I said: it may not come to that. Considering your skill at deception and Page's fondness for you, it probably won't. I spoke of an option. There are no rules in spy-land. You must make them up as you go along," Borya said.

I nodded my head obediently.

"One more thing. Your agent code name is *M1*," Borya said, in a commanding tone.

Sensing that it contained a meaning, I asked why this label was chosen.

"To honor the famed British spymaster *M*?" I asked.

"No. Because *M* stands for *mother* and *1* specifies you as the best. Once this matter is over, I will travel to America. It is long past time for your children to see their uncle again," Borya said, with a smile.

Then, after a tight embrace, he left and I rejoined Alex to mope.

"How did it go?" she asked.

"He felt the need to increase my education," I said.

"He is a great man. There is much to learn from him," she said.

I understood her saying this since Borya was her boss. Still, what she said was true: Borya was a great man and I intended to be a great mother. But as my absence from my children lengthened I increasingly doubted it.

Chapter 74

Thereafter, things happened quickly. Gerald and I were relocated to a two-bedroom suite in the Hotel National on Mokhovaya Street. He noted my relief upon learning we would have separate bedrooms. "Being unwell and snoring loudly, it's best that I have my own room," he said, and I smiled gratefully.

The suite had a Jacuzzi bathtub and attractive boulevard view. It was a pleasant place with an English speaking staff, supermarket around the corner, and closeness to Red Square and the Kremlin.

The hotel's 1903 building contained the charm of lost times with its second floor picture gallery enabling one to feel history. Down the hall from our suite was a sign stating that the President of France had once stayed there.

The breakfast buffet was in the Moskovsky Room where champagne and even soy milk were offered. Being a non-drinking, health-conscious Mormon, I indulged only the latter.

Gerald said that across the street was an excellent Uzbek restaurant we might try. He also suggested that I experience the subway, the Metro entrance being at the hotel's door.

My room was spotless (every mother checks this first), and the Wi-Fi was perfect. My VPN encryption connected quickly, which isn't always the case with public networks. The hotel had a swimming pool and sauna which I didn't expect to use.

After our luggage was delivered, we set ground rules. Though having once acted as a (non-working) call girl, I had never pretended to be married and wasn't sure what to expect. Gerald's words calmed me.

"Our roles require the minimum lovey-dovey: occasionally holding hands but no more. If Page asks why we're not more loving, tell her that being a retired general I'm used to soldierly ways. In the military, affection is forbidden in public as is carrying an umbrella or eating. The only things a soldier can do is walk and salute. I hope to have Valentina and am saving myself for her, understand?" he asked, with a smile.

"Yes, dear," I said, and pecked his cheek.

Chapter 75

Living with Gerald revealed what a happy marital life could be. Mine, with my boyfriend, Randy, had been only occasional despite he being the father of our twins. We had told ourselves that we weren't *ready* to marry, prepared to merge our personalities and needs. We would sacrifice our life for each other or our children but marriage seemed too huge a step.

The truth was that I was more mature than Randy. Becoming a mother does that to you. Though a great playmate for our children, he hadn't yet grown into a parent. This, hopefully, would occur someday.

Gerald *was* grown-up which isn't the same thing as having aged. Or maybe his ex-wife did a better job with him than I had with Randy. Gerald was gracious, considerate, and tried to make our difficult situation work. He assigned me the larger bedroom and always knocked on my door before entering.

What did I do while awaiting marching orders? I read and Face Timed with my family, first warning Gerald so he wouldn't interrupt. Viewing him in the background would raise questions that even my rich imagination couldn't explain.

MARGARET IN MOSCOW

My children excitedly showed me their new toys and paintings. Their grandparents were more courageous than me, permitting the paints and playdough which I barred from my house.

Ever vigilant of surveillance, Gerald and I walked hand-in-hand along hotel corridors and the street. Gerald took me to the nearby Uzbek restaurant, and we rode the Moscow subway.

The Metro has free Wi-Fi, with inbound trains being announced by a male voice and outbound trains by a female voice. A ticket costs fifty-five rubles (about one American dollar) for a ride of any length but transfer to a bus isn't covered by the ticket. Trains pass every one-to-two minutes so there is no need to run to get it. New Yorkers pray for such service even if their subway never closes and the Metro closes as 1AM.

The Metro's elegant walls and ceiling reminded me of Manhattan's Grand Central Terminal. Gerald took me to the Park Pobedy station which is the deepest in the system. The long walk along its corridors and blaring, little understood loudspeaker instructions (my Russian is minimal) made for a surreal experience and I unashamedly gripped Gerald's hand.

We returned to the hotel feeling elated. Mine, from what a tourist gains at experiencing a new setting and Gerald's from the pleasure of revealing it. We intended to dine in the hotel's Beluga restaurant but this plan changed quickly. Upon entering my room, I saw Alex waiting. Spies don't expect privacy so I didn't bother asking how she got in. She looked exhausted.

Chapter 76

"Where were you?" she asked, peevishly.

"Doing tourist stuff: walking and exploring the subway," I said calmly.

Gerald replied to her upset.

"What's happened?" he asked.

Alex didn't immediately reply. Instead, she took off her shoes and tiredly fell into a chair.

"Nothing yet. I've been following Page and her American on their clubbing. They can sleep during the day but I have no such luck," Alex said.

"Where did they go?" I asked.

"You'll see. I'd get some sleep. Borya decided that your initial meeting should be in an informal setting. Alcohol might loosen her tongue so you'll be clubbing tonight and without Gerald. She'll be freer to speak without his presence and since our scenario casts him as aged he couldn't keep up," Alex said.

"Ouch," Gerald said, though with a smile.

"I've never gone clubbing and don't know what to wear," I said.

"We'll check what you have. If nothing's suitable, we'll run out for something," Alex said.

"Let's all nap. You'll have a late night and dozing isn't a luxury at my age," Gerald said.

"You're not *that* old," I said, in true wifely fashion which he immediately picked up.

"Now you can see why I'm hooked on her," he exclaimed, with a big grin.

After Gerald went to his bedroom, I pressed mine on Alex but she insisted on the living room couch. Using a blanket and pillows, I fashioned her a bed. When I looked in later, she was sound asleep with her pistol nearby. I would have preferred being an ordinary tourist.

Chapter 77

Alex regained her energy after napping.

"Let's shop, girl!" she ordered, with the enthusiasm of a teenager holding her first credit card.

I smilingly obeyed, being accustomed to this attitude from my toddlers.

"Where are we going?" I asked, on the way to her car.

"Air Moscow."

"Huh?"

"A fashion boutique for the trendy which you now are."

"OK," I said simply, being unable to think of a reply.

"To begin your do-over for clubbing," Alex added.

"Huh?"

"Yes, all-over. After Air Moscow, jewelry from Saharok in the Patriarch Ponds district. Then to INDEXflat for high-quality Georgian leather shoes, silk t-shirts, cashmere sweaters and a fur jacket, Finally to I AM Studio for what we've missed," Alex said.

"OK," I repeated.

What woman wouldn't have agreed though I had no idea what to buy. I wasn't naïve but had never been to a club. Not wanted to or befriended those who did, Greenwich being an old-fashioned town. Knowing nothing about Moscow nightlife, I depended on Alex who gave me a quick lecture.

"People here dress fancier than in other cities. Grunge is acceptable only in cheap beer clubs. Where we're going, the basic is an upscale suit for a man to image wealth, and skintight dress and heels for a woman to project sex. Tight jeans with a revealing blouse and appropriate shoes are okay. Not looking sexy isn't.

"Muscovites live by the saying that 'clothes make the man.' Dressing well is important everywhere but here you can't be overdressed!"

Chapter 78

Erika, my long-time best friend of a billionaire family, gave me good fashion advice, "Buy simple but the best." So, though deferring to Alex's expertise about Moscow night-life, the dress that I bought had a red, off-the-shoulder neckline with asymmetric length split hem and side zipper. To accord with clubbing expectation an emergency mending had been done, raising one hem to four inches above the knee and the other to nearly five.

"Cover yourself with your jacket when seated," Alex advised.

"*That* advice I never needed," I said acidly.

But Alex simply smiled as we chose my accessories: sterling silver, watermelon tourmaline earrings; silver oval link necklace; Manolo Blahnik stiletto heel, black pump; and a black, crystal embellished, slide-lock closure clutch with a silver chain strap.

"It's large enough for your gun and extra cartridges," Alex said.

"What Moscow women carry instead of lipstick," I said, and smiled.

"*Don't* separate from me," Alex warned.

"That won't work. Page won't speak freely in front of you and there are secrets from our past which I must mention for us to become close again. After introductions, say you're going off to look for a boyfriend. She'll understand and you might be lucky," I said.

"*Lbuov zia, polyubish I kozla,*" Alex said remorsefully in Russian.

"What does that mean?"

"Love is cruel: you could fall for a goat," Alex translated.

We both laughed.

"So where are we going?" I asked.

"*Siberia*, in the Khamovniki District"

"Huh?" I exclaimed, still addicted to this juvenile expression.

"Siberia is Moscow's fanciest club with the biggest Russian stars. It's a good place to talk since there's only a small stage and no real dance floor. The energy level is low because of its nightclub/restaurant combination. Men come to meet stunning models."

Chapter 79

"What time are we meeting Page?" I asked.

"She requested 11PM, the start of Moscow nightlife. She's well attuned to the City's ways," Alex said.

"She a survivor. Don't under-estimate her," I said.

"We're not. Let's take another nap. We may not see a bed till dawn," Alex said.

Page prepared her bed on the sofa and I returned to my bedroom. There, instead of relaxing, I stripped and stood under the shower, a routine that returned my mind to home in America. Suddenly, fear overcame reality and I felt in a fright, consumed by an inexplicable, unnamed dread. *What is wrong?* I asked myself. I had outwitted Page before and could do so again.

I craned my ears and stared at the shower curtain, fearing the knife thrust from without as in the movie classic, *Psycho*. My teeth clenched, my heart walloped, and my breathing became uneven. I stood rigid, waiting for what-ever-it-is to spring but nothing happened. This waking nightmare slowly died as I paced my breathing.

The groundless fright dissolved, leaving me filled with fatigued release.

It had been only my imagination flying in all directions. I was safe in my room with pistol-packing Alex close. I turned off the water, dried myself with the largest, softest bath towel I had ever known, and put on the bathrobe. Still jittery when leaving the bathroom, my eyes moved over the setting, searching for the comforting assurance of familiarity. The king-size bed with wooden headboard. The dressing table with oval mirror. The large window overlooking the Kremlin. All was as expected.

Page was reading on her phone as I entered the living room. She looked up and stared.

"You look drained. Is something wrong?" she asked.

I couldn't speak for several moments. Then, after regaining my senses, I realized what I longed for and need do. I wanted to embrace my sweet children but could not. And knowing like every soldier that few operations proceed as planned, I might never see them again, destined to exist in their fading memories.

Their godparents were good and they would grow up well. They would not have me but, when older, they *could have* my letter.

"I'm all right. I just remembered something I must write," I told Alex.

Chapter 80

I immediately felt stumped. When should this letter be shown to my children? What one tells a toddler isn't told to a teenager. Finally, I picked up the pen and began.

"My dears,

"I looked forward to loving you for many more years but if you're reading these lines, fate has intervened. I had thought of you since our parting, hungering daily for our reunion.

"Yet, duty called. I was asked to aid our country and there was no one else. Why, you will learn from your father. Know this: that despite possible rumor, my mission was approved by the government to help safeguard world peace and for this any single life is secondary.

"Many good people will guide your lives: your father and grandparents and Aunt Erika are just a few. I can give you no more except your remembrance of my love stamped in golden memories. I would have eagerly sacrificed my life for yours were this necessary and, when considering my mission, perhaps I have. With all my love and the hope that fate grants you a far longer life than mine."

After dating and signing the letter, I inserted it into an envelope on which I wrote, "To Be Given To My Children on their Fourteenth Birthday." Then, with it securely packed in my suitcase, I dressed in a fashion markedly unlike my usual.

Alex knocked on my bedroom door. "Ready and coming," I said. Upon seeing me she said with mock severity, "You're *not* ready. No lipstick."

From her purse, she handed me M.A.C.'s Ruby Woo, a vivid bluc-red lipstick. "It's blue base gives the appearance of whiter teeth and a brighter smile. The men will die for you," she said.

After putting it on, I picked up my clutch, feeling comforted by the pistol within. "Better them than me," I said. Alex smiled, thinking that I'd made a joke.

Chapter 81

All that I knew about clubbing came from high school friends who had navigated Manhattan night life. According to them, *face control* existed and formal admission had been required. This was gained by dressing sharp and projecting confidence. I feared failure but Alex reassured me.

"Don't worry. It's been arranged," she said.

It had. Without noticeable signal, she and I walked briskly by the waiting throng and inside. None in the crowd objected. Queues had long pervaded Russian society so a person jumping the line was understood to have official blessing.

Siberia was, as Alex had described, basically a restaurant with a small stage. Expensively dressed men of mid-thirties and older wandered among stunning, younger women hoping for a good deal. It was early for the scene and the crowd seemed a bit stiff. "They'll lose their inhibitions later but business, not partying, is priority at this posh club," Alex told me.

Page wasn't hard to find. She wouldn't be in any club anywhere. There were many beautiful woman here but, on a scale of one to ten, Page is an eleven. Male eyes goggled but, ignoring the stares, she waved us over. While walking self-consciously, I was surprised that many hems were even shorter than mine.

Greetings were brief. I described Alex as a friend, Page introduced me as an "old friend," and her companion was described as an "American friend." With his Brooklyn accent there could be no attempt to conceal his identity.

As conversation lapsed, Alex expressed the desire to mingle and left. Our Act One had opened.

Chapter 82

"It's been *what*? *Three years*?" Page asked, rhetorically.

"Three years," I repeated, grinning like an idiot.

Let her take the lead. She's always been bossy, I told myself.

"*Three years*. How have you been?"

"Working," I said.

Page laughed loudly as if I'd made a great joke. Something about her seemed different but I couldn't place what.

"Yes, and now we're to work together. We've never done that," she said.

"No. Franz suggested it before..."

Mine was a polite hesitancy. Franz had been her past lover and the middle-man who hired her to carry out a killing. in Berlin's Russian consulate. I had worked undercover to discover why. The motive wasn't political but a drug deal gone wrong.

Page avoided prosecution through artful lying and, because a gifted assassin is always in demand, was quickly hired by Moscow's spy agency. Franz was murdered in an alleged street robbery. That his assailant was never caught surprised no one.

Page had been furious when Franz came on to me. Had she *really* loved him? Probably not since supreme narcissists like her only love themselves, I told myself.

"Do you still live in Manhattan?" Page asked.

"Still, though no longer getting work through Svetlana," I said.

Page had gained her New York customers through Svetlana's classy escort service. Following Borya's threat against relatives in Russia, she had inserted me into Page's life.

"Are you still cooking?" Page asked, with a smile.

Happy to be on a safe topic, I returned her smile and said, "Still cooking healthy."

Page turned toward her companion, whose name she hadn't yet shared.

"Margaret is a *great* cook. She shamed me into eating better when we lived together in Manhattan. You can thank her for my passable looks," she said, fishing for an unneeded compliment.

"How many times you need hear you beautiful?" he asked, in a fed up tone.

"It's never enough," Page said.

You haven't changed, I told myself, sighing inwardly.

The man grunted, looking bored, as I held onto my dumb smile. This night won't be worth remembering, I thought, but couldn't have been more wrong.

Chapter 83

Page turned toward the man seated beside her. "This is Larry," she said.

Larry nodded toward me without expression, giving me the sense that we wouldn't be best friends.

I remained silent, not knowing what to say. Glad to meet you, didn't seem appropriate. The silence was broken by the arrival of the waiter who awaited our orders.

"Champagne?" Page asked, turning toward me.

"Bottled water for me," I said.

"*Just teasing*! Margaret is *a Mormon* and doesn't drink! Not even coffee or tea," Page told Larry as if this was hilarious.

Neither he nor the eavesdropping waiter looked interested. Page ordered Krug champagne and the waiter departed. I scanned the room for Alex. She was about forty feet away, speaking enthusiastically with a man and occasionally glancing in my direction.

"Larry and I sometimes work together," Page said, carefully.

I nodded.

"I worried about you after Berlin," I said.

"Things worked out."

"How do you like Moscow?" I asked.

"I didn't until making friends. None as close as we were," Page said earnestly, with a warm smile.

I smiled too since my liking for her was real despite her vocations of call girl and assassin. Developing a growing fondness is unavoidable when living with anyone not totally horrible. And Page had never hurt me though I didn't doubt that she would had she known of my treachery.

"Now we both work for Borya," I said.

"Yes," Page agreed, but tentatively.

This coyness puzzled me but it seemed best not to question it.

With the return of the waiter came the usual bottle opening ritual. During the next several minutes, while I sipped water and they guzzled champagne, we commented on the scene.

"It's too noisy here. We can talk better in my apartment," Page said finally.

I looked toward Alex who was engrossed in conversation.

"Your friend can get a taxi. Come," Page said, rising from her chair.

I instantly followed, ignoring Alex' order to never leave her presence.

Chapter 84

Alex stared as I was leaving the club. She abruptly left her companion but we lost contact in the swarming crowd. Page's car was a black Mercedes. With me seated beside her and Larry in back, she drove like a mad woman, continually bitching about the traffic and more.

"This traffic sucks! A twenty-minute commute in America could take two hours here."

"Why?" I asked.

"The City's twelfth-century plan doesn't work for modern travel. Moscow has four circular rings and many radial roads. The closer you are to the city's center, the denser is the traffic. And because Russian drivers hate rules, there are many accidents and traffic jams. That's why there's so many dash cams."

"Why isn't the gorgeous subway used more?" I asked.

"It is a treasure with its marble veneered stations and murals. But they're incredibly overcrowded during rush hours and there's no air-conditioning. The nearest station for most people is a long walk which is a hassle in winter. And to change lines, you must first travel to the center making for a long commute."

I kept silent as Page chattered, fearing to upset her and increase her road rage and terrible driving but this didn't help. Our journey became even more hair-raising as she drove recklessly through the dense fog. She spoke like a crazy person, repeatedly shouting to the world: "I'll show you!" "Just wait!" "You'll see!"

Yet after parking her personality almost magically changed back into the calm woman I met at the club. Her thirtieth-floor apartment had stunning city views.

"It came furnished. I added a few things," Page said, as she showed me around.

One addition almost stopped my breathing.

Chapter 85

An ebony cabinet bore a large white pentacle in its center. Atop it were three silver candle holders holding unlit candles, three small vases of flowers, an ivory-handled knife, and a thin silver chain. Above the cabinet hung the painting of a naked woman with lightning radiating from her groin.

"What is *that*?" I asked.

"What is *what*?" Page teased, feigning ignorance.

I silently pointed.

"It's an altar."

"An *altar*?"

"You have your religion and I have mine," Page said.

"You weren't religious in America," I said.

"People change and my religion comforts me. Being a Mormon, you should understand."

Her logic was undeniable so I simply said "okay." Page continued speaking while Larry sampled the liquor on the other side of the room.

"Modern witchcraft is a religious fact and not the bizarre hobby of cranks. No one can say how common it is since it lacks the hierarchical structure of other religions. It's large enough to support periodicals and much literature. There are thousands of followers in America.

"Wicca is both a religion and a craft. There is *ritual* and *operative* practice, no different from other religions that seek to help people live harmoniously with the divine principles underlying the universe. Having a nature-based attitude and small-group autonomy, there's no gulf between priesthood and congregation. As a skill, it tries to use psychic means for such good purposes as healing.

"Witches enjoy ritual and are naturally joyous. Like all religious worshippers, they find that proper ritual uplifts and improves. Our rites are more varied than those of other faith, ranging from the official to the spur-of-the-moment and differing from coven to coven.

"But all draw on a shared tradition. The *Eight Festivals* celebrate key points in the natural year such as agricultural, wildlife, and solar. Our festivities put us in tune with these cycles. Our *Samhain*, the thirty-first of October, is your Halloween or All Hallows Eve, and our twenty-second of December is the *Winter Solstice,* days before your Yule."

I uttered "Huh!" as Page paused for breath.

Chapter 86

Page's religious fervor didn't surprise me. She had always been passionate and changeable. Moreover, everyone needs a philosophy of life and it was likely that an assassin needed one too. My uneducated concept of Wicca associated it with Satan. What could Page find more suitable? I asked myself.

She taught me this was nonsense. Wicca is as evil as the Santeria religion which lived comfortably alongside my Mormon heritage. Mother Marie, my Santeria priestess, told me that the Gods aren't jealous.

My phony identity didn't permit me to share this insight with Page. Instead, I listened with larger-than-life interest, wanting to strengthen her trust.

"What I most like about Wicca is that it's a natural, spontaneous religion. One where every coven ("*congregation* to you") is a law unto itself. Nothing is the same in any two and rightly so since otherwise Wicca would calcify.

"There *are* similarities since some rituals, *Casting the Circle*, and the *Legend of the Descent of the Goddess*, are important. Even novices find them moving and nourishing. Spur-of-the-moment additions which a

High Priestess and High Priest bring enhance basic rituals and keep them alive.

"In our urban civilization few *feel* the seasons. Know the psychic tides of the year which made the *Fraternal Rivalry of the Oak King and Holly King* and their sacrificial mating with the *Great Mother* understandable to our ancestors.

"But humanity's archetypes can't be removed any more than can our bones. Though they can be so deeply buried that it takes struggle to re-establish fruitful communication with them. Today, most people's awareness of seasonal rhythms is surface, Christmas cards and Easter eggs. Witches go deeper."

"Wow!" I said, and meant it.

Chapter 87

"Would you like to join our next cover?" Page asked.

Don't accept too quickly. Seem hesitant and make her persuade you, I told myself.

"It sounds scary," I said, hesitantly.

"Scary? For you?" Page asked, mockingly but with a friendly smile.

Page knew me as a call girl who had murdered her rapist father and a cheating customer. That *any* religious meeting could frighten such a person was ridiculous.

"You're right when putting it that way. What goes on at a coven? Who runs the meeting?" I asked.

"I do, here. Foreign cities have more members and High Priestesses with greater power."

"I've called a taxi," Larry said, coming close.

As goodbye, Page hugged him briefly before breaking away.

"We'll talk in the morning," she told him firmly.

When the door closed behind him I asked, "Is he your current squeeze?"

"You must be kidding. He's a thug though clever enough not to be taken lightly."

Is he her operative or intermediary? I wondered, as Page continued my religious education.

"A coven's organization is based on the polarization of psychic femaleness and maleness: working partnerships with one female and one male witch. They may be a married couple, friends, or brother and sister. It doesn't matter if their relationship is sexual. What's important is their psychic gender since in magical working they are two poles of a battery: the High Priestess and the High Priest. *She* is the battery's energy and coven leader.

"Traditionally, the woman is primary with he being the Prince Consort. Wicca is particularly concerned with developing and using the psychic and intuitive powers of the Goddess and to a lesser degree with those of the God though neither can function without the other. Within the Circle the High Priestess represents the Goddess. This is not only Wiccan custom but a fact of nature. Do you know who Carl Jung was?"

I did, thanks to my college psychology class. "A Freudian psychoanalyst before founding his own approach to treatment," I said.

"Yes, and he said, 'a woman can identify directly with the Earth Mother but a man cannot.' That's enough for now. Wicca is a practical religion in which one grows through experience. You'll see," Page said.

What madness have I gotten myself into? I asked myself, as I smiled enthusiastically.

Chapter 88

While Page babbled, I had gradually stopped listening. A person can tolerate hearing only so much about a private universe, which is what Page seemed to inhabit.

I had long before decided that all religions are stories created to enable humans to live a more satisfying life. Mine were the Mormon and Santeria, hers was Wicca, and whatever works for you is fine by me so long as it doesn't interfere.

Mother Marie, my Santeria Priestess, told me of a famed couple on Manhattan's fashionable Upper East Side. He is an initiate of the *Orisha* (divinity) *Changó* (the Santeria spirit of fire and thunder) and she is an inductee of *Yemaya* (the Santeria angel of motherhood, family and the oceans). Together they head one of the largest, most respected houses of Santeria in New York, most of whose members are also Jewish. That such gentle behavior isn't universal had brought me to Moscow.

Page, High Priestess of a Wicca Circle, was believed dangerous, perhaps too treacherous to live. Yet she was a product of her childhood, having been raised by inept parents and raped by her father. Thereafter, helpless and alone, she reacted by using her good intelligence and great beauty to gain independence through wealth. Avoiding the pain of intimacy and longing for the warmth that she never had and feared was too depraved to deserve. I still felt guilty for having betrayed her years before. What would I feel after collaborating in her death?

As Page's words had flowed, an unexpected thought came to mind: the similarities between Wicca and Santeria. Both faiths believe in male and female powers, of everyone having both a mother and father among the angels who punish enemies harshly.

In Santeria, one is not born a witch but with witchcraft powers (*aje*) to be used for good or evil. Being in the right place at the right time, what we call luck, is seen as having strong aje. An antisocial person, one who behaves wickedly, is considered to use their aje toward evil. Then I remembered another Santeria belief: that these witches are thought to be women who belong to groups meeting at night. Women who are believed capable of killing, and even their children. Page?

"*What*?" she asked.

"Nothing," I said sweetly.

MARGARET IN MOSCOW

Without conscious awareness, I had whispered a Santeria phrase in its ancient African tongue: *B'ao ku ishe o tan* (Where there is life, there is still hope).

Chapter 89

Page exaggeratedly looked at her watch: a black, high-tech, ceramic and stainless steel bracelet upon which diamonds twinkled against the clean rectangular dial. A twenty-two-hundred-dollar purchase, she told me. Being rich enough to buy and known to own luxury goods was important to her. I extended the expected admiration though it left me cold. My twelve-dollar watch told the same time.

"It's three-thirty. You'll stay here tonight," she ordered.

Though our rekindled friendship was just hours old, she had resumed her bossiness with me.

"The sofa in this room opens into a comfortable bed. Toiletries are in the connecting bathroom. We'll talk more in the morning," she added, closing the door behind her.

I felt relief, worn down from stress and the late hour, What Alex had said that morning seemed increasingly true: the bliss of normalcy lasts only so long for we drift in a sea of changing currents and depths. Particularly true when considering that my role mere days before had been as homemaker.

It hadn't taken long for the cold reality of that absence to sink in. I missed the touch and smell of my children and the feel of their father's kisses. These will return! I insisted to myself, despite the pervading fear which cheery thoughts couldn't banish. But welcome events followed the next morning as Page's part-time housekeeper arrived to prepare breakfast.

"I ordered a healthy one," Page said, with a winning smile.

Once again, her grace had overwhelmed me and my thanks were fulsome as we ate. Page remembered that I hate eggs and had left off this popular breakfast item. Oatmeal porridge, *grenki* (like French Toast), and the old Russian treat of *sharlotka* (apple cake) made up the rest. We drank milk though Page was a long-time coffee addict.

"I have an appointment and called a taxi for you. We'll speak again before the coven," she said.

She left quickly and I soon followed.

Gerald awaited me in the hotel.

"Alex is on her way. What've you been up to?" he asked, nervously.

"You wouldn't believe it," I said with weary relief.

Chapter 90

"Lie down until Alex arrives," Gerald suggested.

I obliged and closed my eyes. Keeping them shut even after hearing the door open.

"What happened?" Alex asked with concern.

"You wouldn't believe it," I said, repeating what I told Gerald.

Then, regaining self-control, I described the evening.

"Page must be mad," Alex concluded.

"No, prone to instant enthusiasms. Wicca is her latest and it's innocent enough," I said.

"Margaret's right. The general who won World War Two's Battle of Britain became a spiritualist without doing harm," Gerald said.

"What's the American doing here?" Alex asked.

"*That* I don't know. Page described him as a clever thug," I said.

"Is he her lover?" Gerald asked.

"She denied it," I answered.

"You didn't learn much," Alex said, critically.

"Look! I've re-established our friendship and been trusted enough to gain invitation to a coven where she's High Priestess. We may meet others of interest there. I think that's worth something," I said, feeling annoyed.

"I'm sorry. The boss is being pressured so I'm getting it too. Everyone's nervous," Alex said.

"Apology accepted," I said quickly.

"Why did you say *we* may meet others?" Gerald asked.

"Oh, haven't I told you?" I asked, rhetorically. "My friend has also been invited," I said, rendering them speechless.

"*I'm* going to Page's meeting of witches?" Alex asked.

"You are if want to help. Better you than Gerald," I said.

"Another set of eyes would be useful," Gerald agreed, a bit too quickly.

"When is it?" Alex asked.

MARGARET IN MOSCOW

"She'll phone with the time and place," I said.

Then, recalling the nude art on Page's wall, my next statement aroused more speechlessness.

"Don't bring your gun. Nudity seems their style."

Chapter 91

Though not being hungry, I ate following Gerald's military advice to eat whenever possible since your next meal could be far off.

Despite Alex' presence, we had enough of Russian food. I ordered baked salmon for myself and the others chose it too. Apple pie rounded out our American menu. While eating, we considered.

"Why would Page hire an American and who might someone want killed?" Gerald asked.

"My bet is they're American. Page's poor Russian and beauty make her noticeable here. That her accomplice is American supports this theory. Is there any information about him?" I asked.

"He's the youngest, adopted son of a long-dead Mafia chief whose name you probably know, Alex said."

She told us and we did.

"The Mafia is out-of-business. Its heyday was forty-years-ago," I objected.

"True, but he grew up with their folklore. While a teenager he was arrested for small crimes, ordered to attend therapy and given a sealed Youthful Offender record. We learned this informally," Alex said.

"Why not deport him?" Gerald asked.

"That wouldn't help us. We still wouldn't know what's being planned and if he's operator or middle-man. Another person could be substituted and we might not learn who they are. Now we know the identity of two," Alex said.

While snacking on the pie, I raised my persisting concern.

"Why is there so much emphasis on Page? The American could be her old friend."

Alex sighed wearily and turned toward me.

"We keep track of our employee's finances, particularly those like Page who are tasked with sensitive duties. Something unusual happened two months ago," she said.

Gerald and I waited, as if for the heart-stopping climax of a thriller.

"She received a large deposit in her numbered Macao bank account. It worried us and our Chinese source there."

MARGARET IN MOSCOW

"How large was it?" Gerald asked.

"Seventy-five-million-dollars. Enough to pay for a historic murder."

Chapter 92

"She's an assassin," I said.

My statement didn't need elaboration.

"We must learn her target and collaborators," Alex said.

It was more order than suggestion but there could be no argument.

"I'll see what I can do. It may nearly be time for Gerald to do his thing," I said

"What's that?" he asked.

"Nothing dangerous: a restful stay in an out-of-the-way hospital. Page knows me as a fellow killer. I could remind her of my usefulness after suggesting the murder of my elderly, life-insurance-rich-lover who wants to marry me," I said.

Gerald looked intrigued, not startled. As a retired general he had probably heard everything.

"And if all turns out well, Borya will press that Gerald receive our highest medal, awarded by the President himself," Alex said.

"It's a good plan but what about the search for Valentina?" he asked, smiling.

"We're looking. Her mother and husband are dead but she's alive according to records. We're checking with neighbors, showing them an old passport photo which was updated to how she might look now. We won't rest until finding her or information that grants you peace," Alex said.

"I can't ask for more," Gerald said softly.

"Whatever happens, I want you both to meet my children and become part of their lives. Valentina too if fate permits," I said.

"We Three Musketeers," Alex said, firmly, extending her fist.

Ours topped hers in an emotional moment.

Chapter 93

Clichés become clichés because they are frequently true: waiting *is* the hardest. The day before the coven was a bad day for me. I awoke with the horrid, hollow sense which children sometimes have: that of a terror's presence in the bedroom. I feared to extend my foot from under the blanket lest *it* reach from under the bed, grab my ankle, and pull me toward a dreadful end. And I couldn't reach for the lamp switch lest my movement cause *it* to leap.

I battled this feeling like when I was a child and it was just as hard. Elementary fears can persist after maturation, awaiting their chance and nearly getting it. I covered my head with the quilt to not see *it* though the nature of *it* was unclear. As it must be since the real fear lay inside me.

After pulling myself together I tried to reason what had terrified me. Was it that our plan wouldn't deceive our dangerous enemies? A seventy-five-million-dollar payment evidenced serious determination. Or was it that, despite her huge personal flaws, I still liked Page and hated being a factor in her doom. Which was certain if her innocence couldn't be proved.

Everyone worried. Intelligence officials worry when online terrorist chatter is high or low. If high, an attack is imminent. If low, the attack is too important to be discussed online so the message is delivered in person. Was Larry this person? all asked.

To help relax, Gerald took us to eat at a downtown restaurant: *LavkaLavka*. The concierge had recommended it, saying that its staff spoke English.

The restaurant was elegant with great service and a relaxing soundtrack. While eating fish dumplings, I asked Gerald, "What was Valentina like?"

Chapter 94

"What was Valentina like?" Gerald repeated, trying to visualize her.

"When we last met she wore a brown dress with a white collar and a wide black hat wreathed with white daisies. Around one wrist was a gold bracelet that had belonged to her grandmother. With her rosy cheeks, she looked like one of those country girls on old post cards and made the ladies that I'd known before look stiff. My time without her felt dreary, never-ending.

"She was ardent and good-humored though with an infuriating need for almost total independence, maybe from living with a controlling alcoholic husband who beat her.

"For a long time she was indifferent in love-making, maybe feeling that if I learned her body's needs I would try to control her too. But she changed after knowing me better, becoming frank when in the mood.

"There are few things worse than saving things to tell a lover that you never see again. I felt hollow when we split. I shouldn't have let her get away and won't make this mistake again."

Gerald's openness and lyricism had surprised me. One wouldn't expect these from a retired soldier.

"Now, what's troubling *you*?" he asked.

His honesty had made it easy for me to share.

"Living as a single parent with their father being unable to commit is a trial though I'm not sure what caused my terror this morning. Working as an undercover agent has changed me. I know they're professional paranoids and the importance of separating that life from your real life to keep from going crazy. But being normal at other times is getting harder and harder," I moaned.

Gerald grasped my hand before speaking comforting words.

"Life is messy. You're in the middle of a great work and it's chaotic. Keep your level-headedness and spirit and when wanting to flee, bellow to yourself, *which way is the enemy*? Other warriors triumphed at their vital trial and you will too."

Chapter 95

The phone call came early Saturday morning. Not from Page but from a woman who didn't identify herself. I would be picked up at my hotel's entrance at 11PM and driven to the coven, she informed me. Wanting to know more, I asked why the ceremony was held so late.

"We meet at nightfall because the Moon is the light-symbol of the Goddess, standing for the three-fold aspect of Maid, Mother, and Crone who possess Enchantment, Ripeness, and Wisdom. Lunar light provides inspiration for the feast of Brigid, a fertility-bringer and triple Muse-Goddess. She was brought up by a Wizard who multiplied food and drink and turned her bath-water into beer to nourish the needy. When the trumpets sound, spirit and body are quickened."

Even as her words stunned me, an ordinary worry surfaced. Conservative dress is expected at Mormon and Santeria services. What is correct at a coven?

"What is the appropriate dress for this ceremony?" I asked.

"Enticing, with as little as possible," she replied, before abruptly hanging up.

"What does 'dress enticing, with as little as possible' mean to you?" I asked Alex.

"Like it's a congregation of hookers," she predicted.

Which, though we didn't yet know it, turned out to be nearly true.

Few things so clear the mind as spending money and particularly when it's not yours. Needing costumes, we shopped for the basic Russian fashion of high heels and short skirts. Mine was a black, sweetheart-neck, strapless, mini-cocktail dress. Alex' mini had an exaggerated-shoulder and bow-waist fit.

Pointing to a counter, Alex asked, "Now, for the lingerie?"

I shook my head.

"I have a feeling that we won't need any."

Which turned out to be true.

Chapter 96

While awaiting our ride, I paced nervously at the hotel entrance.

"Relax! You have the best roof," Alex said.

"*Roof*? I don't get it," I said, being puzzled by her use of this word.

"*Roof* is Russian slang for being protected by a crime boss or big politician. You're backed by two nations and couldn't be safer," Alex said.

"So why am I so nervous?"

"Because it's you," Alex said.

This was probably true. My tendency to worry became worse after becoming a mother. Still, as a Silicon Valley guru once wrote, only the paranoid survive.

Our driver arrived ten minutes late without explanation. Which wasn't needed considering Moscow's frequent traffic delays. Being the only women outside the hotel made it obvious who we were. She opened the window and called "*vot*" (here).

"A Chevrolet," Alex sniffed.

It was a Chevrolet Niva produced by a joint venture between General Motors and AvtoVAZ, a tough SUV with legendary off-road ability which caused me to wonder at our destination. Though not a Mercedes, it was comfortable enough having look-alike leather seats and a soft linoleum floor.

"Government models are armored," Alex whispered, a statement that didn't increase my comfort.

To relax, I gazed out the window. As the miles sped by, the urban landscape disappeared and the road grew bumpy.

"Where are we going?" I asked, nervously.

"To a dacha forty miles out. We'll be there shortly," the driver answered, in broken English.

I knew that a *dacha* is a country home which could mean anything from a palace to a tiny wooden house. The dacha possesses a sacred meaning for Russians, allowing them to escape city chaos, grow vegetables, and feel free in their private world to rejuvenate with fresh air.

"We won't be picking vegetables," I muttered to myself.

This time it was Alex who said, "Huh?"

Chapter 97

"The typical dacha isn't like foreigners imagine: a wood house with patterned window frames, a babushka in a shawl sitting at the entrance, and tea kettle in the living room. It's usually small and needs repair, without a working toilet but having an outhouse," Alex said.

Hearing this, the driver called back, "Where we're going isn't like that. It's a modern two-story with indoor pool and rooms for guests. It's also well-heated."

Considering my scanty clothes and Moscow having the latitude of northern Canada, it better be heated I thought but didn't say.

"How long have you known Page?" I asked.

"Two months. We met at a party. I'm Leda."

We introduced ourselves.

"How long have you known Page?" Leda asked.

"I'm a friend from New York but haven't seen her in years. Her interest in Wicca is new and for us too. What can we expect?" I asked, with real interest.

"You'll love it. It's more sensible than traditional religions. Which is yours?"

"I was brought up Mormon and Alex had none," I said.

We had never discussed religion but my answer would be true about most who were born before Communism collapsed.

"Tonight's ceremony celebrates the important *February mensis*, the month of ritual purification. It was called *Lupercalia* in Roman times when the priests of Pan ran naked through the streets except for a goatskin girdle. They carried thongs to strike bystanders, particularly married women who were believed to be made fertile by this. The ritual was popular and patrician. Mark Antony performed the Lupercus role and it survived into the Christian era with women stripping themselves to allow the Luperci more scope. The ceremony was banned by a Pope but we value it," Leda said.

"I can't wait! It sounds so honest and sweet," Alex said, with feigned fervor.

Speechless, I stared at her.

Chapter 98

The dacha would have fit into any American suburb but for its high stone walls and security-guarded gate where Leda stopped the car. She smilingly gave her name and the guard slowly admitted the car after a long stare at her bare thighs.

"Rudolf, such a sweet man," Leda twittered once the car passed the gate.

"Does Page own this place?" I asked.

"No, her lover does," Leda said.

That explains the security, I thought. Corruption and crime had flourished after the fall of Communism. Business disputes were settled with guns and armored sedans became popular though inadequate when the car bombings began. Things became calmer after the election of President Putin but Moscow still lacked the order of American cities.

The front door opened as we approached, having been announced by the guard or video surveillance. Leda embraced our greeter and introduced us. Tatiana was tall and appeared younger than me. She wore a pale blue sheath which extended barely below her pubis. Her ready smile didn't stop my discomfort at her tight embrace which I reserve for my children and boyfriend. Sensing this, she pulled back.

"I'm sorry. We're a small group and appreciate each new member," she said, apologetically.

"Don't think about it. I didn't have the best parents and tend to be uptight," I lied.

"Except with her customers," Alex added.

It's safer to be believed a whore than a spy, I thought, joining in their laughter. But I couldn't help wondering what I'd gotten myself into.

"The ceremony begins in a few minutes. You'd best get changed," Tatiana said, ushering us down the corridor.

Chapter 99

An odd feeling arose as we walked the long hallway. Though Tatiana had been friendly, something about her unsettled me. What is it? I asked myself, and then it came. Her knowing eyes set into a child-like face whiffed of corruption and appalling practices. What have I gotten myself into? I wondered again.

We entered a bedroom of Japanese décor. A Shoji screen with black lacquered framework and translucent panels formed a sleeping alcove dividing the room. Its style was magnified by the vertical lines of the bamboo window covering. Looking carefully, every surface had a different texture but, far from conflicting, like the subdued colors they blended pleasantly making the room feel serene.

"Ceremonial gowns are in the closet. There's an adjoining bathroom to freshen up," Tatiana said, and pointed.

The elegant bathroom was of contrasting fashion. Almost spacious enough to entertain in, its black and white tiles added an Edwardian feel to the his-and-hers basins, each with an overhead light and mahogany-framed mirror and shelf. The period-style painting of a nude woman added a classical touch, and icing champagne bottles lay in an open cooler. Close by the toilet was a bidet with a built-in douche spray. In a corner was a shower enclosure with etched glass doors.

"This is *some* bathroom," I said, with frank admiration, thinking to remodel those of my Greenwich house.

"Boris, Page's lover, is an unusual man," Tatiana said.

No response was expected or given. I chose a gown and stripped.

Chapter 100

Including Alex and me, the coven consisted of nine, all dressed in the same blue garb which would force stares and maybe arrest in many cities. Men would love them.

Like the bathroom, the ceremony room was in 19th century Victorian style with sturdy wood chairs, overstuffed sofas, and thick carpeting. Burning logs in a formidable stone fireplace was the center of attention. Alex and I observed from a sofa, awaiting the activity which Page began.

"Spring-cleansing is upon us. At Candlemas, all Yuletide decorations must be burned: holly and ivy and mistletoe, even the sweet-smelling bay and rosemary box tree. If not, gremlins will haunt the house," she said.

"A newness of life is here so we must rid ourselves of the past and look to the future. Today's stormy weather means Winter is over; fine weather on Candlemas day means more Winter is coming. Candlemas is the turning-point between Winter and Spring and to be impatient about it is unlucky."

Page pointed to two women.

"The High Priestess selects two woman witches who, with herself, represent the Triple Goddess: Maid (Enchantment), Mother (Ripeness), and Crone (Wisdom). Prepare the Crown of Lights!" she ordered.

A woman sprang forward to light birthday-cake candles above a firm copper crown. Its foil cap protected hair against dripping wax though these candles hardly drip. Other equipment was a small bundle of straw dressed in a doll's dress, and a thin, pine-cone tipped branch with black and white ribbons spiraling along the staff. These lay beside the altar with two unlit candles in candle-holders, a small flower bouquet for the woman who portrayed the Maid, and a dark-colored scarf for the Crone. A broomstick and evergreen twigs lay by a cauldron holding a burning candle.

Though feigning entrancement, it all felt like high school drama. I would have preferred to be reading in my hotel room but that wasn't why I was in Moscow.

After supplication to the *Great God Cernunnos*, the witches (including Alex and me) danced back-to-back in couples with arms hooked through each other's elbows. When Page decided this lasted long enough, she stood at the altar and prayed aloud," Dread Lord of Death and Resurrection, Of Life, and the Giver of Life; Lord within us, whose name is Mystery of Mysteries."

She raised her wand to invoke a Pentagram of Earth in the air and said, "Blessed Be."

The rite finally ended with the burning of the evergreen twigs, removal of the Crown of Lights from the Mother's head, the Maid laying down her bouquet and the Crone her shawl beside the altar. We then shared cakes and wine. Thus, for the first time in her life, did this Mormon taste alcohol. She needed it.

Chapter 101

The later conversation was conventional: opinions about Moscow's best hairdresser; Yandex Taxi's new ride-hailing helicopter service; and the renaming of Russia's airports after famous residents with Moscow's Sheremetyevo Airport to be called Pushkin Airport.

"Witches, Boris needs this room for a meeting so it's time to leave. Cars and drivers are outside," Page ordered, before hugging each of us.

Alex and I changed though the others simply put on their coat for the ride back. Being costumed like a whore grated on this mother.

"What did you think of it?" Alex asked.

"It's innocent enough. Page isn't being paid seventy-five-million-dollars for Black Magic," I said.

"No."

Upon leaving the bedroom, we nearly collided with three men in the corridor. One wore a three-piece gray suit with white shirt and a blue necktie with a white figure. Another wore a chocolate-brown suit with a white shirt and a tan necktie. They looked important but far less than the man in the middle.

My best friend, Erika, bought her widowed father's clothes for him before his remarriage. Being of a billionaire's family, she purchased only the best. I had often accompanied her on shopping trips and knew this man's clothes were expensive. In contrast to his two companions, he was casually dressed in a navy blue sport shirt, quilted vest, and burgundy jeans. None of his outfit could have cost less than six-hundred-dollars and his vest was probably double that.

While his face was handsome, his eyes made him unforgettable: glowing eyes which narrowed when he spoke. Sinister, knowing eyes. They passed without recognizing our presence.

"*Boris?*" I whispered nervously to Alex, and she nodded.

Chapter 102

Four cars waited outside. We and two women piled into one. We remained silent as they chattered.

The ride was smooth and steady, thankfully absent of traffic jams. Before entering the hotel, I tipped the driver and waved goodbye to our fellow witches.

"It's late. Stay with me," I suggested, and Alex didn't argue.

Gerald had waited up for us and I quickly filled him in.

"It sounds innocent enough," he declared.

"That's what we thought except for Boris," I said.

"Who's Boris?" Gerald asked.

"Page's oligarch boyfriend. He has the most evil, knowing eyes. Just seeing him creeped me out," I said.

"Because Page is Boris' lover is why Borya hesitates to act against her," Alex said.

"And what if he's involved with her scheme?" Gerald asked.

"*That* decision is beyond Borya's pay grade as Americans say," Alex said.

"It's way past bedtimes. We'll talk in the morning," Gerald said, as I yawned.

Despite the quiet, well-heated room and comfortable bed linen, I couldn't sleep. The evening's activities had disturbed me though they'd been peaceful and its members sweet. It was seeing Boris, I decided. His black, knowing eyes.

I had seen similar eyes before, on a Mafia boss who I was trying to hire to protect a college friend in jail. During our drawn-out negotiation, I forced him to take me seriously by pointing a pistol at his stomach. But this understanding didn't relax me. Thinking about my children did.

Chapter 103

Though nothing had changed, I still felt better in the morning which is how things can go. Even so, there was nothing for us to do but await orders or for something to happen. The others noticed my glumness.

"You look miserable," Alex said, over breakfast.

"I'm tired. Playing a role is exhausting," I said.

"It should be over quickly. These things have a life of their own. Just when you're sure nothing is happening it does. You note a thread and where it leads and things start making sense," Gerald said.

"Seventy-five-million-dollars' worth of sense?" I asked.

I instantly regretted my surly tone. Gerald was an expert and much older.

He didn't reply but touched my hand supportively.

"I'll check with Borya to see if anything is new," Alex said.

That's where matters stood until Page phoned me that afternoon.

"How did you like the coven?" she asked, brightly.

"It was almost *too much*," I said, in Valley Girl breathless pose.

"I was afraid it might have been, popular ideas about Wicca being of Salem witch trials and all that though Wicca is simply more nature based than other religions. What you saw was a normal Irish Spring rite of a thousand years ago, not me on a broomstick."

"Oh, did I miss that?" I asked, with a laugh.

"*That's* at the next coven. I didn't want to overwhelm you," Page said, lightheartedly.

"The others were nice," I said.

"They are. We're all working girls."

I knew what *that* meant.

"Come to my apartment at four. Alone, so we can talk freely," Page said.

After hanging up, I turned toward the others.

"Things are in play," I said.

Chapter 104

I felt calmer once things started moving, having been jumpy since leaving America. Leaving my toddlers was hard as was traveling to mysterious Moscow and adopting the identity of call girl. I worried how Page would react to me, which was important considering her skill as an assassin.

But Moscow proved charming, as had my confederates. And things seemed to have gone well with Page though only time would tell.

Page wasn't a Wicca Princess at our next meeting where we shared personal happenings.

"Are you involved with anyone?" Page asked.

"I'm nearly married," I said.

I had never seen Page speechless before but my announcement did it.

"*Married?*"

"In a while, briefly I hope."

"That must be a story."

Which is what I told her.

"Gerald fell for me. He's nice apart from snoring loudly and being forty-years older. He says he isn't well and has a heart condition with maybe five years to live after which I'll inherit."

Page looked sympathetic. Eliminating awkward people was her business.

"What are you planning?" she asked softly.

"Marriage, and his reaching Heaven a bit sooner," I said, sweetly.

We understood each other perfectly.

Chapter 105

"Helping is a two-way street. I help you and you help me," Page said.

As if her statement had unquestionable logic, my reply was a simple nod to show I was listening closely.

"You're weren't happy working in the business were you?" Page asked.

"It chose me but was a living."

"How would you like being able to retire?"

"That wouldn't be possible even after Gerald died. His pension stops at his death and his house is heavily mortgaged. Child support and alimony took him to the cleaners after the divorce, and his life insurance isn't that much," I said.

"Like I said, I help you and you help me."

I let the silence build before speaking again.

"We're alike, like blood-sisters in a cobwebby world," I said.

"Whatever I would do, you would do," Page said.

"That's what I always thought," I said, with feigned sincerity.

My statement brought Page up from her seat and close to me on the sofa.

"I'm going to tell you a secret. I have a well-paying project and need an assistant that I can trust. You'll make more money than you ever dreamed, enough to retire on. Are you interested?"

"Of course."

Then, knowing that greed had always been her biggest motive, I asked, "How much are you talking about?"

"What would you say to five-million-dollars?"

I could have said that it was only a small part of what she had been paid but didn't. Instead, I said, "I'd do anything for that."

"You must be free to travel. A husband would be in the way," Page cautioned.

"But not for long," I said.

We exchanged smiles.

Chapter 106

"My lies seem to have a life of their own with me going along for the ride," I told Alex the next morning.

"That's how it is working undercover. Is anything new?" she asked.

"Page hired me as her assistant for five-million-dollars. I haven't been told my duties except that it involves travel so Gerald must die," I said.

"*You have been busy,*" Alex said admiringly. "I'll tell Borya and alert Gerald to his murder. I hope he gets a laugh."

"She hasn't told me how. A phony Moscow newspaper obituary would convince Page and not disturb his American relatives," I said.

"Thus dies another marriage," Page said, with a smile.

I didn't find her comment funny and she noticed.

"*What?*"

"I do want to get married," I said.

"What's the delay? You're a great woman. Is your boyfriend crazy?" Alex asked.

I smiled appreciatively at the needed compliment.

"Just one of those men who takes time to grow up. I hoped that having children would speed this up but it didn't. Don't misunderstand me! Randy is great with the kids but marriage doesn't seem a word in his vocabulary," I said.

"Maybe your absence will make him realize how much he needs you."

"That could be the problem. We've been a couple for ten years but might fit together too well though he needs a strong woman like me to manage his life."

"What's wrong with that?"

"I sense his resentment. After getting his doctorate he might decide that what he really wants is the exciting life he missed, one with another woman and without parenting responsibilities," I moaned.

"He can't be that stupid."

"Oh, but men certainly can," I said bleakly.

Chapter 107

Though Page's activities held far greater importance than my boyfriend problems, I couldn't shut up. I *had to* examine this issue and Alex was there.

"Whenever I've raised this issue it leads to unsettled interchanges. Randy, how would you feel about getting married, I ask. Fine, he says. No, how do you *really* feel about it my darling? I ask. If it's what you want, it's what I want, he says, which isn't exactly a ringing endorsement. No, I want to know how you *feel* about it especially since it means settling down. Can that be the rub? I often ask myself.

"I think of giving up but having a life without Randy feels shocking, as unbelievable as placing our children for adoption. Playing house with someone else is out of the question since he *is* what my life is about. Having him as partner and lover makes sense out of life's chaos."

I abruptly shut up, having needed to air my all to an understanding audience. And though Alex couldn't solve my impasse, I still felt better.

"We must sometimes make a choice which shapes our future: to leap or let the opportunity pass. Things will probably work out with Randy. Having survived together so long signals that, despite everything, the bond holding you is powerful. I wouldn't be gloomy. As you said, it takes more time for men than women to grow up."

Then, unexpectedly, my thinking shifted far afield.

"Holding a memorial service for Gerald after his death would assure Page of my sincerity, particularly if it's attended by officials. I'll write an address," I said.

"I'll arrange the setting," Alex said, nodding approval.

Chapter 108

Speaking with Alex had helped me recover emotional balance, absorbing the lesson that flowing with the current is the way to go. An hour after Alex left to arrange Gerald's service, I clued him in on his part.

"I first met Page in New York. My mission was to become her chum and I did. She believes me to be a call girl who murdered two people. To further convince her of my identity, you might have to die," I said.

"Huh!" Gerald said.

My juvenile speech habit is contagious, I thought frivolously.

"But your murder is justified since I need the freedom to travel," I said.

"Making me deserve my fate. My death will be painless, I hope," Gerald said calmly.

"*That* I haven't learned. Page is the expert on such things."

"You will tell me."

"Of course, and try to make sure that I do the killing."

"Please do more than try," Gerald said.

Which was a reasonable request lest things go real.

"Your funeral will be closed casket and I've written the commemoration. Would you like to hear it?" I asked.

"It would be a unique experience."

I theatrically opened my laptop and read slowly.

"To speak honestly of Gerald is difficult for the truth would be hardly believed. Those who knew him will believe my words small while the outsider will consider them exaggerated. Having overcome oppression and hardship, he made it his life's mission to safeguard America's freedom, living with the confidence and courage.

"America's freedom was purchased by men like Gerald, soldiers who sought not fame but respect. Their merits exist in eternal memories of all who associate joy with freedom and freedom with heroism.

"My words cannot reduce our sadness at losing Gerald, the grief from losing a good we have become used to. Our memories of Gerald cannot dim for he owned the best of qualities and was the finest of men. From our sorrow comes insight and self-control."

As I finished speaking, my eyes blurred with tears though I didn't know why.

"Getting a memorial speech like that makes my death almost enviable," Gerald said.

I visualized the scene.

"What creed do you want the clergyman?" I asked.

"Whichever would gain me entrance into Heaven," Gerald said, with a wry smile.

Chapter 109

Time seemed to slow while awaiting Page's phone call and our anxiety and impatience grew. There can be paralysis by analysis when fear and crippling doubt grow. Borya phoned Alex daily and Andrew, the American Counterterrorism agent, called me every evening.

"Maybe Page decided on someone else," I said.

"That's unlikely. It would take time to find another trusted person. She'll call," Andrew predicted.

Then, as if his words had gone directly to Page's ear, she phoned.

"Come for dinner tomorrow night. Dress casual, it'll be just Boris and me. He wants to meet you before leaving for Sochi," Page said, in a commanding tone.

"Okay, where?"

"At the dacha. My car will pick you up at seven."

A voice in the background was followed by Page's muffled reply. Then a friendly "SeeYa" before she hung up.

Gerald and Alex had been watching me intently.

"It's dinner tomorrow night, to meet Boris at his dacha. She's sending a car," I told them.

Alex asked the question on all of our minds, "Is he involved?"

"I might learn. Where's Sochi?" I asked.

Alex' tourist information lowered the tension.

"Before the fifty-billion-dollar 2014 Olympics, Sochi was a Black Sea beach with a swampy coast serving migrating birds. Posh infrastructure changed it into the gold-plated brilliance of ritzy hotels in European-style town squares with restaurants and Western brands. A thirteen-hundred seat concert hall is planned," she said.

"Maybe he'll tell me about it," I said.

"We'll hope more than that," Gerald said.

Chapter 110

When nervous about a forthcoming engagement, a woman's thoughts naturally turn to what she'll wear. After searching through the clothes that I brought from America, casual, as stated by Page, became for me a Saint Laurent black silk striped blouse with full button front, single button cuffs and rounded hemline, and black J Brand Natasha high crop skinny jeans with exposed button fly and five pocket styling.

"Chic, but will your gun fit in the pocket?" Alex asked.

"Do you think I'll need it? What's the rule on these assignments?"

"Following rules is convenient but not always safest. Having a gun beats one left at home," Gerald said.

With this in mind, I added an Akris pink silk and cashmere jacket with patch pockets. The PSS silenced revolver fit within.

"*Now* you're dressed for battle," Alex exclaimed.

"If it comes to that, I've already lost," I said.

A half-hour before my ride was to arrive, I rehearsed my identity with Gerald and Alex.

"I'm a call girl who murdered her rapist-father and a client who tried to stiff her. Being greedy, gaining Page's five-million dollar payment is my goal which I'll do anything. Have I left anything out?"

"Say that learning about Wicca strengthened your desire to retire which her payment will make possible. That you feel yourself aging and don't want to wind up giving blow jobs in alleys," Alex said.

I nodded agreement as her words awakened an unrelated worry: not wanting to live my whole life as an unmarried parent.

Chapter 111

I must have looked nervous for both Alex and Gerald tightly hugged me before I left the hotel room. In the over-heated lobby, I watched departing guests bundled against the cold and thought warming thoughts.

That day, after speaking with my toddlers, I had talked with my younger sister, Melanie. Being an ambitious teenager, she increased her allowance with earnings from babysitting the children of wealthy Greenwich families.

Back in my day, which now seemed ancient, babysitters were hired by personal reference and scheduled well in advance. Now in the new gig economy, parents logged onto an app and hired them on whim. "It's an Uber for babysitting," Melanie said.

I had never heard of it and was intrigued.

"How does it work?" I asked, with motherly curiosity.

"Better than you might expect. I only go to families that dad knows so I leave his gun home."

"*What?*"

"Kidding. The real danger is getting comfortable with a lifestyle I'll probably never have. The people hiring are rich enough to book on a whim, sometimes only a few hours' notice. They have stylish hair and expensive watches, introduce the TV remote and their child in that order. I indicate on the app when the job ended and if it's after 11PM I get taxi fare. Payment shows up in my Venmo account."

"It's different from my babysitting days," I said.

"That was when our family was poor, isn't it?"

Melanie referred to when my father was disabled by Lyme disease and unable to work.

"Yes. We're still glad those years are over," I said.

"So you know what it's like in these mansions with the fanciest baby stuff and massive TV with all the channels. The kitchens have dishwashers and refrigerators disguised as cabinets. Why are rich people so ashamed of appliances?"

"Beats me. I don't hide mine," I said.

"You're not rich."

Oh, I am. Years before, using Randy's hacking expertise, he and I stole twenty-three million dollars from a German crook. But this isn't something that Melanie should learn, I thought.

"I try to get jobs where the child will be sleeping so I can do homework or watch Netflix or talk on the phone. And though nosey like you, I don't peek in drawers or closets. There could be small video cameras recording and interesting secrets are probably well-hidden anyway."

"The jobs sounds great. Any objections?" I asked.

"Well, one mother said their babysitter usually did the dishes."

"What did you do?"

"I washed the dishes. I'm a very cooperative person," Melanie said.

"Mom might not agree," I said, with a laugh.

"I don't expect that she would," Melanie agreed, in a surprisingly adult tone.

Chapter 112

Mentally replaying my conversation with Melanie had a calming effect. The driver called my name and courteously opened the rear door of the black sedan. The interior was warm and, before reseating himself, he took off his jacket to reveal many tattoos. Neither of us spoke and I occupied myself with watching the fading city lights and studying his tattoos.

Alex had told me their history. When the Communists ruled Russia, prisons were controlled by a gang known as the Thieves in Law. They enforced guidelines about prison tattoos with each telling a story of brutal crimes or of standing up to authority. Undeserved tattoos were forcibly removed and followed by beatings.

The Thieves in Law rules are no longer followed. Now, inmates create their own images with varied meanings. The driver had three visible tattoos. One was a rose wrapped around a dagger. Alex had told me that this symbolized a person who was first imprisoned before the age of eighteen. His tattoo of a snarling wolf (an *Oskal*, for "big grin") indicated having hostility toward police. His shoulder tattoo, a dog with bared teeth, specified bitterness toward life.

MARGARET IN MOSCOW

I was no longer ignorant about Boris' business dealings. His driver's tattoos had told me everything.

Chapter 113

Dinner was just the three of us. Boris' casual dress softened the dining room's artful décor where traditional style met modern. He pointed out the Zhipeng Tan table, the Jeff Zimmerman chandelier, and the 1790s chalk-painted French armchairs. A pale-blue ceiling kept the room light and airy.

Pointing to a painting, Boris remarked, "The artist said that a failed painting is better than a simply bad one because the failure might have been great. One could say that of some life opportunities too." Is this Boris' subtle employment invitation and way of saying that he isn't just a crook? I wondered.

Nor was the meal what I expected for the buffet consisted of the Americanized version of Chinese delicacies: Egg Drop Soup, Shrimp and Bean Sprouts, Vegetable Fried Rice, Egg Rolls, and Chinese Eggplant with Spicy Garlic Sauce. All perhaps chosen for me, an American semi-vegetarian.

During dinner, Page told stories about Wicca. I found them fascinating but Boris' eyes glazed. Obviously, the stories were intended for me.

"Many popular ideas about Wicca are nonsense, like that of *witch cake* made from dried scorpions, toads, snakes, and ground puppies."

"*Please*, we're eating," Boris ordered, though with a smile.

Page nodded obligingly and turned toward me.

"Have you heard of being hexed?" she asked.

"Having an evil spell placed on you?" I asked.

"Yes, and the greatest hex murder trial occurred in America," she said.

That got my attention.

Chapter 114

"Witchcraft was the heart of the murder with headlines about witches riding broomsticks. Most no longer believed in evil hags who killed babies and plagued sleepers for fun but some did. Troubled, sickly, young John Blymer lived in a rural community. His calling was faith healing which was also called *pow-wowing* and witchcraft. It involved making spells with things like a lock of hair and blood.

"*Pow-wowers* could supposedly place a spell on someone. Many blamed their illnesses and those of their farm animals on bewitching and Blymer had hard luck. He followed a popular, old-time spell book, *The Long Lost Friend,* which advised on problems like worms and stopping bullets and catching thieves. To stop bleeding you breathe three times on the cut, pray the Lord's Prayer three times, and say The Three Highest Names three times."

"What are The Three Highest Names?" I asked, as Boris yawned.

"Beats me," Page said, continuing her story without losing a beat.

"Though weird and a loner, Blymer finally found a wife but she left him after their two babies died and he lost his job. He had problems sleeping and eating and became convinced that someone had hexed him. His father-in-law thought he'd gone crazy and had him committed to an institution which he left without anyone noticing.

"He soon found two teenagers who also believed they'd been hexed. Their families' crops were failing and animals were sick. Blymer went to a pow-wower who confirmed that he'd been hexed and named a man named Rehmeyer who did it. To break the spell, a lock of Rehmeyer's hair had to be taken and buried.

"The three young men went to Rehmeyer's house to investigate. He admitted to having a copy of the witches' Bible, *The Long Lost Friend*, invited them to spend the night, giving them a good meal in the morning. Convinced that Rehmeyer had hexed them, the men later returned to his house and killed him while battling to gain his hair and witch book."

Noting my rapt attention, Page returned to sipping her soup to increase suspense. She had mine!

"Well?" I asked, feeling irritated.

MARGARET IN MOSCOW

Other friends behave the same and it always annoys me.

Chapter 115

"The crime scene was awful. A fire was set to conceal the murder and Rehmeyer's body formed a charred nightmare of bone, blood, and ash. But the house was intact since the killers had closed the door tightly, keeping out air that would have spread the fire and the victim's body fluids snuffed out his funeral pyre.

"Having been seen by a neighbor, the men were soon arrested and placed on trial. The prosecutor tried to explain the crime as a robbery gone wrong and leave out anything about witchcraft but couldn't since one man confessed, 'I got the witch.'"

"Rehmeyer's hair hadn't been snipped since with his death the hex was considered broken. Each man blamed the other for the killing blow and all were convicted with two getting a life sentence and the third getting ten to twenty years.

"They did well in prison, now feeling secure. One was a gifted artist and created vital maps during World War II. After his release, he painted portraits for local families. Another married, was a church volunteer, and retired from a factory job. The central character,

Blymeyer, was a quiet prisoner who worked as a janitor and night watchman after prison.

"We do *nothing* like this and are entirely innocent," Page said, concluding her story.

"You were never innocent," I said, playfully.

"Nor were you," she responded.

We all smiled as if being members of the same guild. But Boris' smile lacked humor, seeming that of one who rarely laughed.

Chapter 116

Though trying to look relaxed I felt nervous as I remembered Borya's story of what Russian Air Force instructors tell new fighter pilots: to always check their six o'clock. Six o'clock is directly in back of them and twelve o-clock is looking straight ahead. They're not safe until checking their six-o'clock, the trainers continually advise.

Was I safe? I asked myself. Did Boris or Page know who I really am? Boris' smile seemed false but he didn't appear the sociable type. I would watch my six-o'clock but only time could tell. As the dishes were cleared and beverages served, Boris turned toward me.

"Tell me about yourself?"

"There's not much to say. I grew up in the American mid-west. Page and I shared an apartment in New York."

"You're both *whores,*" Boris said, cruelly.

Obviously, tact wasn't in his nature.

I don't usually blush but his comment forced it. And though my identity as prostitute was sham, I felt angry. No woman likes being called a whore. But my voice was calm and controlled when I spoke.

"The last man who called me that died unexpectedly," I said.

"Tell me about it," Boris said.

Now his voice was soft and caring, an appeal for honesty.

I didn't respond instantly, wanting him to think that my judgment of him determined what I would reveal.

"I've had a hard childhood. My father's rapes didn't stop until I killed him. Years later, a customer called me a whore and tried to stiff me. This would have made another rape and wasn't going to happen."

"Did the killings bother you later?" Boris asked, with a comforting touch of his hand.

"The world is better off without them. I slept the sleep of the angels," I said.

My voice was tough, without humor. Now, Boris' smile was real.

Chapter 117

"I had no choice. My poverty smelled of corn chips, dirt, and my father," I continued, almost spitting the words.

My drama had taken on life.

"I nearly gave in to anger, gave up on myself. Having a father who raped me and a mother who wouldn't notice if I'd been raped in front of her. I survived but not completely. I still have flashbacks and some odors pull me back to my father's bed. My childhood had its own rules: steal what you must and don't get caught was what I learned best. Taking was done to me and what I did later."

"How did you kill your father?" Boris asked, with the emotionless tone of a psychologist.

I thought quickly. My mind was on a roll.

"It wasn't hard. While the others were away and he lay drunk, I held his gun in his hand and pulled the trigger. Suicide was common in my town."

"You've suffered far too long. We'll help end it," Boris said.

MARGARET IN MOSCOW

What most surprised me weren't these tempting words but his caring tone and that I suddenly liked and trusted him. This, though knowing that those in his business are professional liars.

Chapter 118

Dinner ended late and Page suggested that I stay the night. I agreed, feeling comfortable since I sensed that nothing sexual was involved. Not with Page since she didn't go *that* way nor with Boris since I detected his disinterest. Power seemed his motive and I wondered how much intimacy existed between him and Page. Collaboration but possibly little more, she being a useful tool which he also hoped for me.

While intelligence officials worried, we watched an old black-and-white movie from a huge modular couch with multi-position electric mechanism. "The movie is one of Boris' favorites," Page whispered.

This surprised me though it needn't. *Everything* about him had been surprising. He wasn't the typical thug that I expected.

I hadn't doubted his intelligence or toughness: one doesn't become or survive as a billionaire without these traits. What did surprise me were his magnetism and complexity, like the central character of *Shadow of a Doubt*.

Seeing the title had shocked me for it was one of my favorites and of my film-loving oldest sister too. We had seen it so often that we repeated some of the dialogue. Its twisty plot might characterize the currents of Boris' life, I thought.

Shadow of a Doubt tells of Uncle Charlie, a serial killer and robber of wealthy elderly women. While under suspicion and watched by New York City detectives, he flees to California where his older sister lives a small town life with her husband, teenage daughter, Charlie, and two younger children.

Changing residence is easier than changing habits and Uncle Charlie targets a rich lady as the detectives arrive. Told of their suspicion, teenage Charlie helps them, this placing her life in peril.

Look to your six-o'clock, Borya had advised me. Did Boris' choice of movie hint his suspicion of me?

Chapter 119

I discreetly focused on Boris as the movie unfolded. Uncle Charlie's escape to California. His enthusiastic welcome by family members and particularly his niece, Charlie, who bore his name. The arrival of detectives disguised as magazine photographers, seeking Uncle Charlie's photograph to identify the killer of elderly women. Teenage Charlie's growing suspicion and the murder attempts on her life.

Boris' hard face had smiled during these scenes. I had earlier noted the veins in his cheeks and nose, the curling gray hair at his neck, his thick eyebrows and dark-rimmed eye sockets. His eyes concealed a quick brain and he typically spoke with a voice that was bad-tempered to the point of hoarseness.

Though nearing sixty, his energy was of a much younger man despite having slow, deliberate movements like those of an invalid. Page said he could work without sleep for days.

The movie ended with Uncle Charlie's death and teenage Charlie's budding romance with a detective. Boris slowly rose and suggested that we retire which we did.

"It's a *wonderful* movie," Page said, when we were alone.

I agreed, keeping the fact that I had already seen it to myself, following Borya's advice to "reveal as little true information as possible."

"Come schmooze in my room," Page suggested.

I did, wanting to strengthen our friendship and increase her trust. As we sprawled in pajamas and robes, Page asked, "What do you think of Boris?"

"He's impressive. I can see why you're with him," I said.

"As a boss, not much *that* way," Page said.

"Huh!"

"*What*?" she asked.

"I assumed you were lovers."

"*You're* the oversexed one," Page said, and laughed.

I laughed too though sex with my exam-wracked boyfriend had been infrequent.

"So what do you think of him?" Page repeated.

MARGARET IN MOSCOW

"He's sharp," I said.

"He's much more than that."

My quizzical look gained only a repetition.

"*Much* more."

Chapter 120

Sleep didn't come easily as my mind was consumed with the evening's events: the movie, Boris' personality, and what Page meant by "much more." What would seventy-five- million dollars purchase? Elimination of a business rival? Murder of a head of state?

Page had played big, risky gambles before, once assassinating a drug king-pin inside Russia's Berlin Consulate. But, relatively speaking, that had earned her peanuts: a few hundred thousand dollars. These stakes must be far greater.

By morning, Boris was gone and we left after a hurried breakfast. "I'll clue you in later," Page said upon leaving.

Back in the hotel, Gerald and Alex bore in before I'd removed my coat.

"Well, what happened?" Alex asked, tensely.

I excused her abruptness, knowing the pressure she faced.

"We watched a great old movie but you're not interested. Boris is into something big," I said.

I knew these details wouldn't satisfy them. They didn't satisfy me.

"I didn't learn what. Page said she'd clue me in shortly."

"What's your impression of Boris?" Gerald asked.

"He has an almost feminine intuition about people. What surprised me is that I found myself liking him though he also revolts me. His eyes have a magic that makes it hard to turn away, as if he senses greatness in himself and awaits his turn to the throne. There's a large painting of him in a marshal's uniform that he keeps glancing at."

"He's never been in the military," Alex said.

"I know. I read his background and it makes me uneasy," I said.

From my pocket I removed the Derringer that I had been provided and asked Alex, "Can you get me a PSS to go with this toy?"

Chapter 121

I became the target of hard stares

The PSS is a six-shot, 7.62mm silent pistol, far more effective than the two-shot Derringer I held. It is used for clandestine scouting and killing. Once, in Tokyo, I had carried a Stechkin silent revolver with the same caliber but less powerful cartridge.

"Things are that menacing?" Alex asked, without surprise.

"One doesn't take a knife to a gunfight," I said.

This had been the advice of my German stepmother who was a celebrated agent before retiring to domesticity.

"You'll have it," Alex said, simply.

Silence weighed until she turned to Gerald and spoke. "Now for the good news. We've found Valentina."

Delight lit our faces as we awaited details.

"She's healthy and lives in Moscow. Her daughter works as an airline stewardess. We've told her nothing about you, saying that we were checking eligibility for her late husband's pension. Do you want to see her?"

"Do I want to see her? Of course I do!" Gerald cried.

Then, moments later, he spoke softly, "I'm afraid."

"Well, you won't need a PSS for that," I said, trying to be supportive through humor.

Though it wasn't much of a joke, Gerald smiled and our discussion turned to whether their initial meeting should be deliberate or made to appear casual, and how best to re-introduce himself?

Doubtless beneath these concerns lay Gerald's unspoken fear: What becomes of my life if Valentina isn't interested? I raised this issue gently, in another of my made-up stories. Hoping to be helpful despite being so much younger.

"Before my present boyfriend, I had an earlier lover. We were joined at the hip and planned our future: the wedding, even names of our children. His family moved and he went with them but I couldn't get him out of my mind.

MARGARET IN MOSCOW

"Two years later, using my father's credit card, I impulsively bought a plane ticket and went to see him. When I showed up at his door, his parents remembered me but he barely did. All were polite but puzzled and I quickly left, older and wiser as they say. Feeling a goner until meeting Randy, the father of my children. Maybe you fear the same," I said.

Chapter 122

Earlier in my life I would have felt uneasy advising someone so much older but no longer did. Being a mother had given me a confidence and certainly which I previously lacked. Giving birth is a difficult, brilliant achievement and I did it. My toddlers thrived thanks to me. Okay, I also had supportive parents and friends and an always available doctor. But it was *me* who did it so speaking firmly to Gerald had been right, which he felt too.

"Thank you, I needed that. It's been decades since Valentina sped away in a taxi and we're both very different, I remember her as she was and she'll do the same. Still, like they say of people my age, if you're still walking around you're doing good," Gerald said.

Our merely polite laughter recognized that a compliment was sought. Every mother can identify this motive.

"Stop it, Gerald. You're an attractive man! I've seen woman give you the come-on. They don't approach because they're sure you're with me and not as a father," I said, firmly.

Gerald smiled though not believing me. His were normal dating jitters make worse by special circumstances. When meeting Valentina he would be calm. We returned our attention to his initial task.

"I would phone her first. She wasn't hard to find so that you did won't seem odd. Say you're in Moscow for a conference, are looking up old friends and she was the best of them," Alex said.

"And wing what you say from there," I added.

"I've dreamed of you for decades. You were my greatest love," Gerald said, with twinkling eyes.

"You can't beat *that,*" I said, firmly.

We all smiled and relaxed.

Chapter 123

Gerald reached for his phone to call Valentina. Fearing that our presence would increase his anxiety, we exited our live soap opera for the breakfast buffet in the Moskovsky Room.

Nibbling on cheeses revived my appetite but the offerings were wonderful too. After several trips to the buffet table, I turned toward Alex.

"Dealing with Boris and Page is like being in a dark unending tunnel. Causing me to shiver with fear but knowing that only I can find the way out," I said.

Emotion boiled through me and I felt like crashing my fist on the table but didn't. Thinking was the intelligent thing to do and only it could save me.

"We must do things differently, study the situation as if we were scientists not detectives. Detectives move from clue to clue before piecing it together. But clues can add up to the wrong picture too.

"We must approach this logically from the lowest point. See where the wires cross and study the design, approach the problem from all angles, then turn it over to view it microscopically.

"The creation of life reflected a long, erratic chemical reaction but this setup is occurring under controlled, predictable circumstances and can be stopped."

"What are you saying?" Alex asked, looking confused.

Pulling my thoughts and courage together, I said, "Boris' goal isn't more money. It's to take over a nation."

Chapter 124

Alex chewed a piece of *grenki* (like French Toast), thinking. Finally, she spoke.

"You're talking big stuff," she said.

"Very big."

"Which makes sense. There've been rumors..."

I felt as if I had chosen to cuddle a poodle which turned out to be a starving attack dog.

"What rumors?" I asked.

"Undercurrents. Odd, coded messages, increasingly frequent meetings, unneeded military drills to takeover civilian targets, not defend them. Now it all fits together and makes sense," Alex said.

"I hope I'm wrong."

"So do I but Borya must be told," Alex said.

She abruptly got up and left.

A waiter hurried over. "Was the food satisfactory?" he asked kindly.

"Perfect! It couldn't be better. My friend remembered an appointment,"

My explanation reflected excessive courtesy. Becoming a mother had forced me to set good examples for my children.

Gerald's romance lost importance. A coup in nuclear-armed Russia would be an earth-shattering event. By the time he and Valentina met, the world could have turned on its axis or the human race been extinguished.

Gloomy thoughts stayed until optimism took over. What's most feared is the unknown. A creaking board at night, a sudden voice on a supposedly deserted street. But now things made sense and the enemy was known.

Boris was like the snake lying unseen, fostering others' grandiose Napoleonic dreams and dousing their fears. The hidden one who assured that feet weren't dragged during action, the power behind the throne.

He was a fanatic but not a fool, needing concealment to be effective. Helped by Page, a politically naive assassin who would follow orders. But even the craftiest snake could be spotted as it slithered through the dust.

MARGARET IN MOSCOW

Unable to further endure the room's joyful crowd,
I left as a question crowded my mind: Was Boris' scheme
detected too late?

Chapter 125

It has been stated that one who writes their biography is committed to lies and cover-up but I have tried to write the truth even when it wasn't favorable.

After sharing my conclusion about Boris, I felt myself immersed in an imaginary world having no bearing on my real life. Yet also knowing that this was an innate security mechanism, one intended to sanction my doing whatever was needed and resolving to succeed.

Things began looking changed. There were now more police about the hotel, a site favored by foreigners. But Gerald wouldn't have noticed for his mind was on Valentina and their first phone call. Listening to his description returned me to my high school days when I empathized with the emotional romantic tumult of friends.

"We're meeting tomorrow," he said, excitedly.

"Where?"

"At Erwin RekaMoreOkean, a restaurant beside the Moskva River at Kutuzovsky Prospekt. The concierge said it's lavish but reasonably priced. Its specialty is fish caught in Russia. I felt she might have become vegetarian like you," Gerald said.

"She'll appreciate your thoughtfulness. Mention it."

"Thanks, I will."

Hoping to not greatly lower his mood but knowing he must learn, I repeated what I'd told Alex.

"It makes sense," he calmly agreed.

"Be careful outside."

"Always, everywhere, though the streets should be safe. A coup would need a communications takeover. The recent one in Turkey failed because the plotters didn't do this first. I'd start worrying when you can't make a phone call or the internet goes down. There was an old movie about an American military coup, *Seven Days in May*. Boris' play seems the same."

"What happened in the film?" I asked, with more than casual interest.

"The coup leaders backed off when their plot was discovered. No one was hurt and news of it was buried to not upset the public."

"Hopefully, fact will follow fiction here. It's not yet May," I said.

Gerald managed a weary smile to my playful comment.

Chapter 126

While treachery and corruption are part of the human kind, so is love. Valentina phoned Gerald to say she had a headache, seeking a rain check for the following day. This may really have been anxiety, which was reasonable considering that their last date had been decades earlier.

Gerald agreed, later asking me if he should offer to go to her house to help. I suggested this was too early in their new relationship and he didn't go.

Alex brought the silent pistol that I requested and I re-familiarized myself with it at a public shooting club in Moscow's Western District.

To avoid questions about the unusual gun, Alex had a uniformed policeman accompany us though she needn't have bothered since her credentials would have been more than enough. By tradition, security officers are studiously avoided by Russians.

The other range patrons were the typical fun-loving people that one meets in Western shooting clubs. Here, all type military weapons could be rented with the preference being a Kalashnikov (AK-47) assault rifle.

After shooting it, customers were given an AK-47 key ring, a typical sales pitch of theme parks.

"If you want, we can go next to a club where you can fire an anti-tank missile," Alex said, as I reloaded.

I turned to her and stared.

"I'm not joking, it's available. Maybe when everything is over," she said.

The paper targets offered ranged from the image of a non-threatening animal to a pistol-aiming bad-guy, which I chose. The *splatterburst* target caused a bright yellow hole to appear where hit. The instructor checked our eye and hearing protectors before we entered the range.

The PSS-2 is a small (six and one-half inch), light (twenty-five ounce) six-shot, recoil operated gun with an effective range of seventy-five feet. It is termed *silent* since the cartridge contains both an internal piston and a propelling charge. Upon firing, the charge projects the bullet from the barrel while the piston seals the cartridge neck to prevent blast from escaping.

Though having been described as a gifted shooter, I hadn't fired a weapon in years and it took a while for me to get up to speed. Shooting rapid-fire, my first six shots, aimed at the bad-guy's upper chest, went low. But all bullets from the next three magazines were killing shots, hitting his upper chest or head.

"*Not bad.* But with only six rounds in the magazine, what'll you do if you're facing many shooters?" Alex asked.

"I run," I said, without even the trace of a smile.

Chapter 127

Valentina's "recovery" was swift and their next date went off as planned. It was important that we witness it for though being entangled by love, Gerald was also on a mission. Valentina might be an innocent but we couldn't be sure, being ignorant of Boris' allies. Thus, decency be damned, we watched and listened as the lovers cooed.

Valentina had told him that she would be downtown shopping and it would be easiest to meet for lunch at his hotel.

"Russians consider all Americans rich. She might be ashamed of her apartment," I suggested to Alex.

"Or because there's suggestion of a lover," she rejoined.

"You're *so* suspicious."

"That's why your uncle values me," Alex said.

Thus, not unlike mischievous schoolgirls, we spied on their date. Not by peeking but with the latest eavesdropping equipment. The waiter captain smilingly obliged, encouraged by a hefty tip and Alex' SVR credentials. "It's a matter of state security and not to be revealed," she ordered.

Earlier, Gerald had been unsure what to say.

"Is Valentina a spy?" I asked.

"Certainly not!"

"Then tell her the truth: that you're a divorced, lonely grandfather who came to Moscow mostly to find her. You're also meeting scholars for your next book but if you had to choose, you'd spend all your time with her. When asked how long you're staying, say it depends on her."

Gerald digested this silently.

"It does," he said, finally.

"It also depends on Boris. By next week, bullets may be flying and we all could be sheltering in place," I said.

"Like during every battle when lovers cling and parents pray," Gerald said.

"*This* mother can't stop thinking about that," I said.

Chapter 128

I offered to make their reservation at the Beluga, the hotel's high-class dining room. Gerald's approval simplified installing the surveillance equipment, with the waiter-captain placing them in a quiet corner.

Noted for its Russian delicacies and luxurious caviar bar, the restaurant would impress Valentina with his prosperity, an important consideration for their first date.

"I'll stay in my room to avoid the risk of comment by a hotel worker," I told Gerald before he left.

"Good thinking."

"And keep our adjoining door locked, just in case you understand," I said, in a mock-serious tone.

"I should be so lucky. Things don't happen quickly at our age. The talk tends toward grandchildren and Beano," he said.

"Oh, no!"

"You'll see someday."

MARGARET IN MOSCOW

When he left, I went to the room which Alex had reserved for the surveillance feeds. We waited and waited and, just as we feared Gerald had been stood up, saw them being seated at their table. Valentina was so good looking that likely the last time any man had said "no" to her she was in diapers. The casual clothes and ring on her finger was the female version of camouflage, of not wanting to be noticed. Her beauty was youthful lushness altered by maturity.

She was dressed in black trousers, a white blouse, and an elegant grey jacket. She looked radiant and Gerald gave her an adoring look. Sensing that their date would work out fine, I didn't want to see more but Alex insisted.

"We're being vigilant, not lewd," she insisted.

She was correct and I watched too.

They chatted in English and Valentina's was flawless. Despite Gerald's flip comment to me, they didn't mention Beano but did speak of his children and her hope that her daughter would finally settle down.

"Her latest conquest is an Air Force Major. He's serious about her but she's independent and uneasy about being a soldier's wife," Valentina said.

"I'll have him checked out," Alex instantly remarked.

"Now, tell me about yourself: what brought you to Moscow?" Valentina asked.

Gerald took her hand and spoke an ardent "You!"

"You're sweet but what else?" she persisted.

"She's checking him out too," Alex interjected to me.

"A conference about the Battle of Stalingrad, which saved Mother Russia and Western civilization too," Gerald replied to Valentina, in a serious tone.

Chapter 129

Hearing the word "Stalingrad" caused distress for Valentina. The video feed was so good that her tearing was visible.

"Many of my relatives died there," she said hoarsely.

Stalingrad was the pivotal clash in the war against Nazi Germany. Until Stalingrad, the Nazi armies appeared overwhelming. After, their defeat ended in a devastated Germany but its cost was huge. For five months, ten German armies charged eleven Russian armies causing nine-hundred-thousand German casualties and two-million Russian.

These figures don't reveal the complete horror. Nearly cut off from food, Stalingrad's residents died from disease and malnutrition. Pets disappeared into the food supply and reports of cannibalism were widespread. The Russian victory aroused an almost miraculous sense of hope among the depressed Allies and Stalingrad's valor became an enduring memory for all Russians.

"What do your scholars say about the battle?" Valentina asked.

"That victory came through exceptional Russian courage and self-sacrifice. Bombed-out streets were turned into fortresses with one apartment building, defended by twenty-four soldiers, remaining uncaptured during a three-month assault. But that the Germans lacked resources too: hungry soldiers can't last."

Silence followed Gerald's monologue, it taking time for Valentina to regain calm. They then caught up on each other's lives: Gerald's divorce, the death of her alcoholic husband and her guilt at feeling relief when he died.

"Our romance marked me too," Valentina said, grasping Gerald's hand.

Alex turned from the screen and phoned for Room Service.

"We've seen enough," she said.

Chapter 130

I stayed out of our suite just in case. Even the thick hotel walls couldn't avoid hearing lovemaking from an adjoining room.

Gerald had become a father-like figure for me and hearing parents make love is a no-no. Nor will I ever occasion this for my children. I did calling: to my children and their grandparents who were caring for them, and to my German father in Berlin. Being told that he had just left for the airport, I spoke with Ulrika. Though they weren't married, I had long considered her a true step-mother.

"He'll be sorry to miss your call. There's a meeting in London he had to attend," Ulrika said.

"Did he fly from the new Brandenburg Airport?" I asked.

I wanted to keep our conversation light, seeking relaxation before returning to battle.

"It *still* hasn't opened. Did you hear the story?" Ulrika angrily asked.

"No."

"This is it. Brandenburg was intended as a state-of-the-art airport to mark Germany's comeback as a global destination. It cost billions and should have opened in 2012 but that date came and went."

"What happened?"

"An example of how *not* to do things from the allegedly super-efficient Germans."

I said nothing and Ulrika continued.

"Brandenburg now has an impressive main terminal with no passengers, huge empty luggage carrousels which must be kept moving to keep them from seizing up, and a connecting railway station running one empty train a day to keep the air moving."

"What happened?" I repeated, being unable to stifle a laugh.

"Changing travel choice and people happened. Politicians with no talent for management made continual changes while construction was going on. The airport's architect hated shopping and wanted few stores but the airport company insisted so they had to be crammed in along with essentials like sprinklers. Little capacity was included for low-cost flights which became popular. 'It's like fixing an airplane's mechanics during flight,' an expert said. There were literally a half-million complications."

Learning that disaster makes my obligation seem easy, I thought, as Ulrika stopped to draw breath.

Chapter 131

"Isn't *anything* good happening in Berlin?" I asked.

"I won't say it's good but Communist restaurants have become the rage."

"Huh?"

The word burst from me before I could stop it. A mother shouldn't use juvenile expressions I kept telling myself.

"Yes. Eateries from the Eastern Bloc's Cold War past have arisen. They specialize in cheap hearty meals in rooms with Stalinist-era posters of heroic workers and soldiers."

"Huh!" burst out again.

Can using this expression be genetic? I wondered.

"Customers enjoy the silly thrill from being both Communist and exotic but our family won't eat the food if I have anything to say."

"What is it?"

"Combined German and Korean. Think of cow tripe with kimchi and Korean blood sausage with pig's liver. Not the thing for a vegetarian like you or us since Vladimir's heart attack."

"How's his health?"

"Much better since he swore off all fast-food. He's lost weight and recovered his energy. He vows to last until having grandchildren," Ulrika said.

"Bully for that!"

"How's your family doing?" Ulrika asked.

"The kids are healthy and my adoptive father has become famous as a Connecticut Supreme Court Judge. His re-election is certain and its changed his life."

"How?"

"When working as a lawyer, people spoke to him freely. Now they seem to fear being jailed for saying the wrong thing. Which is nonsense since even if he did have that power he's probably the kindliest judge on the bench."

"It's long past time for our children to meet. When would be a good time?" Ulrika asked.

"I want that too but aren't sure. I'm in Moscow, helping Borya," I said.

Ulrika had formerly been an agent and knew Borya. I didn't have to explain.

"Can I help?" she asked.

I felt touched by her instant offer to leave her family to aid me.

"Bless you, but no. I have help and with luck will be home in a few weeks," I said.

Her final comment didn't improve my mood.

"One shouldn't rely on luck too often," she said flatly.

Chapter 132

I returned to our suite the next morning. Bad tempered and deciding that Gerald and Valentina deserved no more than one day's intrusion into my personal comfort.

I needn't have inconvenienced myself. During breakfast, Gerald told me that, after their lunch, Valentina rushed off to bid her daughter goodbye on her return to work. They made another date for that day. Sex had reared its head only psychologically, if at all. "We're not teenagers," Gerald said, offering an unneeded excuse.

Suddenly, an unrelated thought came to mind: no belief can be so wrong as one created by oneself.

"What's the matter?" Gerald asked, noting my upset.

"Is it obvious?"

"Pretty much. Are your kids okay?" he persisted, this being the initial question of every parent who looks anxious.

"They're doing fine, missing me but well. It's about Boris. He must be doing something hugely illegal considering Page's huge paycheck but I can't help liking him. What if my mistaken belief forces action. Russia doesn't have America's legalities. When the government feels threatened, people are killed or disappear into prison," I said.

"Like with any government under attack. We're not talking fraud but something that could affect millions of lives," Alex said defensively.

"Facts are needed to confirm my theory," I said.

"That's your job," Gerald said.

Knowing he was right, I changed the subject.

"How did things go with Valentina?" I asked.

"I don't know," Gerald said, slowly.

Alex and I waited for more.

"We probably hoped to begin where we left off decades ago but life doesn't offer that. Then we were both miserably married without seeming exit. Now we're free and must discover if we're really right for each other. Freedom can be scary."

Both noticed my sudden change of expression.

"What?" Alex asked.

"*Freedom can be scary.* Boris said it too, that Russians fear freedom and yearn for a dictator,"

"Few Russians would want a Stalin or Hitler as ruler," Gerald said.

"Not if they had a choice," I said, gravely.

Chapter 133

Every investigation has a key event. A statement or happening after which things swing one way or the other. Here it was a video that Boris showed. *Before*, I questioned his guilt. *After,* my doubt disappeared.

This happened on the following weekend, the preceding days being filled with more chatting of romance.

"Do you want to marry?" I had asked Gerald.

This was a more than casual question since my boyfriend's reluctance to marry had kept it fresh in my mind.

"I'm not sure. At our age it doesn't seem important and it's too soon to raise the issue with Valentina," Gerald said.

"I might never marry," Alex said, firmly, as if she already thought this through.

My Russian father never tires of telling me the importance of family to Russians so her declaration surprised me. Gerald was surprised too.

"Why not?" he asked, in a curious, uncritical tone.

I earlier considered Alex only as a security officer. Now I realized she had philosophical beliefs too, and the capacity for wisdom which not everyone has.

"When people ask a dating couple if they're considering marriage it's like asking if they're serious about their relationship. Marriage is seen as critical for a successful life, the best solution to the deep human desire for belonging and doing so is almost deserving of a medal.

"But it comes with a cost. My married friends have become narrow-minded, less likely to socialize and to help even relatives with things like errands and transportation. Do I really want a life so isolated? For now I've decided 'no' but who can say about the future. Craving children would make a difference but also that I'd have to retire to a desk job which isn't me."

"One's personality makes a difference," Gerald said, pensively.

I nodded but said nothing.

Chapter 134

"Nations can progress through their disasters but we can't afford to fail. The stakes are too high," Gerald said. Then, as if it were an afterthought, he turned toward Alex and asked, "What is Borya really like?"

Borya was central to our mission, the King Spider's strands watching Boris' intrigue. Though my often-jolly uncle, he was Alex' boss so it was best to ask her. But Gerald's question had placed her in a difficult position: talking about an employer is risky unless only favorable things are said.

Yet this wasn't what we needed. An intentionally glossy assessment would risk our lives since as important as knowing your enemy's resources is knowing those of your allies. After a lengthy silence, Alex replied.

"Borya is more coach than a boss in the popular sense. I consider him a generous, empathetic, principled captain, one who forms a communal enterprise with his employees though with spurts of cursing.

"He seems to view his workers as a team with his role being to maintain its energetic, aggressive tempo. He admits his mistakes, treats us like adults, and sometimes even hands us the reins. By abandoning his ego, he makes it easier for us to set aside ours and police ourselves.

"He's not the self-absorbed star who assumes he should be boss because he's the most talented. Instead, he stays aware of everything, relying on others when recognizing that he can't shoulder it all. He doesn't behave as if believing that a leader's job is merely barking orders to be blindly followed but sees himself as part of an intricate dynamism where his workers harmonize their behavior to form the most potent organization. He respects us and we respect him."

Alex had spoken gravely and the ensuing silence recognized this.

"We will trust him," Gerald said, finally.

I was proud to have Borya as a relative but, perhaps from caution at the approaching events, felt the need to say one thing: "I hope that while battling monsters we don't become monsters ourselves."

Chapter 135

Thinking back, what most stood out about Boris was his frequent appearance of knowing things that he wasn't telling. Borya was like this too though also very different. He would never enjoy *that* film nor shown it to us as Boris did.

But this happened later, after a week during which the only thing new was the deepening romance between Gerald and Valentina and my increasing boredom. Since Borya had ordered us to remain close by, we stayed in the hotel and I became bored and prickly.

"Clearly, you're a mother missing her kids and boyfriend, wanting to go home but unable to leave," Alex said.

"You're right. What should I do about it?" I asked.

"Talk to them on the phone. Then we watch a romantic movie," Alex said.

"Sounds good to me," I said, reaching for my phone.

My twins spoke excitedly about their newest toy, shared complaints about each other and of their recent fun trip. Randy moaned about having to write his dissertation twice and being told by his advisor to re-write it again. After an hour spent providing an attentive ear to my toddlers and encouragement to their father, I turned to Alex who had been eavesdropping.

"Who supports me?" I asked, wearily.

"Me, of course. Let's watch a movie," she said.

We did.

Chapter 136

Thanks to the internet, watching a movie was no longer the hassle as during my childhood when I had to choose from among the few at my local Greenwich theatre. My oldest sister, Melody, was always a good companion though our tastes differed. She liked depressing European films and I liked lighter ones. We usually compromised with a classic of Alfred Hitchcock or Federico Fellini at the Greenwich Film Society where she volunteered. We had already seen most of them but, like good sex, they can't be experienced too often, Melody told me. This was well before I confirmed that piece of sisterly advice.

The movie I chose was the Hitchcock classic, *North by Northwest*. It's a romantic thriller starring Cary Grant, the undeniably handsomest actor of another era. The plot has a New York advertising executive being mistaken for a foreign spy, this placing his life in danger. Along the way he interacts with a mysterious beautiful woman in scenes filled with double-entendres. During heart-stopping scenes he's on a field avoiding bullets from a crop dusting plane, and hanging from a mountain ledge facing a killer's pistol above.

MARGARET IN MOSCOW

"That was *wonderful!*" Alex exclaimed, after the movie ended.

I grinned and was about to say something when Page phoned.

Chapter 137

"What's up?" I asked.

"You'll learn Saturday. We've been invited to Boris' apartment for dinner. I'll pick you up at seven. Bring overnight stuff," she said, before abruptly hanging up.

"I've been ordered to an overnight at Boris' apartment on Saturday," I told Alex.

"Which one? He owns several."

"I don't know. Page is picking me up," I said.

"An overnight. Be careful."

"Always."

While waiting I tried to relax but couldn't, attempting to prepare though nothing could be done.

"You can never really relax," Alex advised me. "The actual operations are the high spots but the waiting becomes a bind. It takes something out of you each time there's a phone call or knock on the door. You're always thinking of your story, modifying it to fit fresh circumstances with foolproof reasons for being wherever you may be or was discovered. The real trick in this game is knowing how to use what turns up."

I dressed as a high-price whore with heels, tight clothes, and elaborate makeup. Page picked me up similarly dressed. Would more than companionship over meals be demanded? I wondered but didn't ask.

"You'll love the apartment. It's nothing like the slum we shared in Manhattan," Page said.

Our pricey apartment had been better than was inhabited by most Manhattan residents but I said nothing. Still, Boris' apartment was special.

It had multi-zone air-conditioning and underground parking, a three-sided layout that included a kitchen-dining room, a large living room with terrace overlooking Moscow's historical center, four bedrooms and three guest bathrooms. The master bedroom had a fireplace, its own bathroom, and a dressing room. The kitchen had Miele and ZUG appliances.

"When does my pay include an apartment like this?" I asked, with feigned overstated eagerness.

Chapter 138

That Page possessed the key to Boris' apartment told me something about their relationship. But the hug that he gave her was restrained, perhaps because of my presence, and I received the same.

Boris had ordered that dinner be served upon his arrival and this was done. The cook was Russian and the food was marketplace Chinese: shrimp and bean sprouts, wonton soup, eggplant with spicy garlic sauce, and fish and broccoli. All appreciated by health-nut me. When I remarked on this, Boris explained.

"I try to please guests but also to lose weight. It's easy to gain when you're older," he said.

Boris provided the conversation and we the audience. Dialog isn't expected from whores. He described a church choral concert that he recently attended and read from its program.

"The song's words are from an American Shaker tune. They were an eighteenth-century sect who believed that Jesus would return to judge the world so they had better be ready. Men and women were separated in different villages and led celibate lives, living simply with few personal possessions. They were supported by sales from their furniture workshops, sharing their songs with the public since the celibate church survived by recruiting new members," Boris said.

"There wouldn't have been call for our skills," Page said, with a seductive smile.

Boris gave her a nasty glance before reading from the one-hundred-fifty-year-old song text.

Tis the gift to be simple, 'tis the gift to be free,

Tis the gift to come down where we ought to be,

And when we find ourselves in the place just right,

Twill be in the valley of love and delight.

When true simplicity is gained,

To bow and to bend we shan't be ashamed,

To turn, turn will be our delight,

Till by turning, turning we come round right.

Upon concluding, Boris' expression was peaceful, like that of a clergyman blessing whores.

Chapter 139

When dinner ended, drinking began, it quickly changing from champagne to vodka. Russians are notorious for their alcohol tolerance, their repeated toasts during negotiations being a weapon since refusing to drink is considered insulting. Page matched Boris glass for glass and explained my abstaining.

"Margaret is Mormon. She doesn't smoke or drink, not even coffee or tea," she said, in a nasty tone.

I understood. She had feared her boyfriend's attraction to me years before and now my possible appeal for Boris. But her remark only increased Boris' interest.

"You don't drink at all?" he asked, with seeming disbelief.

"It's a family religious thing. Self-control is so much part of me that drinking alcohol scares me if this makes sense," I said.

"It does. Have you read the ancient Greek philosopher Epictetus?" Boris asked.

"No."

He left his chair to select a book from the bookcase. After leafing through pages he began reading.

"You would fain be victor at the Olympic games, you say. Yes, but weigh the conditions...You must live by rule, submit to diet, abstain from dainty meats, exercise your body perforce at stated hours, in heat or in cold; drink no cold water, nor, it may be, wine. In a word, you must surrender yourself wholly to your trainer, as though to a physician.

"Count the cost and then, if your desire still holds, try the wrestler's life. Else let me tell you that you will be behaving like a pack of children playing now at wrestlers, now at gladiators; presently falling to trumpeting and anon to state-playing, when the fancy takes them for what they have seen. And you are even the same: wrestler, gladiator, philosopher, orator, all by turns and none of them with your whole soul.

"Like an ape, you mimic what you see, to one thing constant never; the thing that is familiar charms no more. This is because you never undertook aught with due consideration, nor after strictly testing and viewing it from every side; no, your choice was thoughtless; the glow of your desire had waxed cold.

"Friend, bethink you first what it is that you would do, and then what your own nature is able to bear.

You must watch; you must labor; overcome certain desires; quit your familiar friends. Weigh these things fully and then, if you will, lay to your hand; if as the price of these things you would gain Freedom, Tranquility, and passionless Serenity."

"Epictetus was renowned for his wisdom," Boris concluded.

After closing the book he gave me a thankful look and I intuitively glanced at Page. Her face reflected barely controlled fury.

Chapter 140

The bedroom assigned me was ornately decorated with thick rugs and drapery, bedside antique lamps and clock, and large carved headboard and footboard. There was a makeup table and mirror but, surprisingly, nothing contemporary. Not even the enormous digital television common to bedrooms of the super-rich. Was this Boris' idea or his decorator's? I wondered.

Pleading fatigue, I turned in as their drinking continued. This wasn't an excuse since I was exhausted. Page's increasing hostility and the stress of role-playing had gotten to me. I feared forgetting my lines and saying something catastrophic like referring to my children. Even my vivid imagination wouldn't disentangle me from *that* mess. Thus I followed my mother's long-past advice to leave a dicey situation before disaster occurs.

Once in my room I scrubbed in the shower as if to rid myself of the unpleasant evening. Then, after admiring my shape in the long bathroom mirror (thinking, *not bad for a mother of twins*), I dressed in the see-through negligee I'd brought.

Aided by a long steaming shower, I immediately fell asleep until awakening to a soothing voice. Half-asleep, I imagined it to be my boyfriend. Luckily, I didn't speak his name since it was Boris. Being fearful, I had left the bedside lamp on.

"Did I wake you?" he asked.

He obviously did but I played along.

"It's all right. I had been thinking about what you read from Epictetus," I replied.

This wasn't true but I sensed it was the right thing to say. As Borya never tired of repeating: "An agent's survival comes from following their instincts."

"What struck you?" Boris asked.

"His insistence that victory is gained by surrendering to your trainer, following their advice as one would their doctor's," I said.

My instinct again proved correct. Boris nodded and smiled.

Chapter 141

Boris' tone was soothing, his chilling philosophy envisioned to be swallowed without consideration.

"People need leaders who must remain distant since authority lacks prestige without distance. Being confident in his judgment and conscious of his strength, the leader makes no attempt to please and all that he asks is granted."

I tried looking entranced despite his authoritarian jargon, arrogance, and political hunger. These had led to the horrors of Hitler and Stalin.

"People need freedom from complex decisions, to concentrate on family and work without the political decadence surrounding us. You look stunned," Boris said.

"It's a lot to take in all at once. What you say makes good sense but you're only one man," I said.

"A man can fell a mountain with the right help and helpmate by his side," Boris said.

Though having failed as middle-school actress, I tried to put on an adoring look. But my lack of talent didn't seem to matter since I had been chosen as Boris' helpmate and he saw what he wanted.

"Page?" I questioned.

"She is useful and beautiful but dumb. My helper, never a helpmate," Boris said.

I instantly understood. But Boris' hope of taking over the government required far more than two addle-headed women. I need learn his allies but appearing curious was risky. "Don't ask questions. Let the facts flow," I had been instructed. I waited silently.

Boris pulled back the comforter, removed his robe, and joined me in bed. He was naked and stank of alcohol. He bit my earlobe as his hand rhythmically massaged my groin. My order had been to play-act a whore but need I be one too? Boris thought so.

MARGARET IN MOSCOW

Chapter 142

I had already considered whether, while role-playing a whore, I would have to be one. I fantasied how it would feel, having had only one boyfriend in my life. Randy and I had an emotional bond which I wouldn't have with a stranger. But did this matter with so many lives being at stake? Thousands perhaps millions, including those of my children.

But it didn't happen with Boris that night for, after more harsh gropes, he just lay beside me and spoke, unable to perform likely because of the alcohol.

Sergeant Alamo, a family friend and Greenwich police detective, once said that many criminals talk. Even those who had been previously jailed and knew the value of silence couldn't stay quiet though lying before telling the truth.

He said that he understood why a murderer would confess. Taking another's life is such a haunting experience that if they don't tell someone they'll explode inside or ghosts will appear.

He said nobody gives you the whole story right away. It comes out in trickles until most emerges though a little is held back. Maybe the silly stuff like after ax-murdering the guy he crapped on the floor.

I remembered this when Boris spoke. I was now considered his helpmate, his accomplice in a looming crime of stunning magnitude.

"Only just Page and me couldn't accomplish it," I objected, in my best Valley Girl tone.

"You could with Val," Boris replied.

Though unable to see his face since it lay on my breast, I sensed his grin for I knew about Val. It wasn't a person.

Chapter 143

Val is a silenced assault rifle used by Soviet special operations forces. Originally designed nearly forty-years before, its latest SR-3 Vikhr model stock makes it ideal for concealed carrying.

The gun fires a 9X39mm round that can penetrate body armor at up to twelve-hundred feet using a telescopic or night vision sight. A selector switch enables firing in single round or automatic mode. I pretended ignorance since the Val isn't common knowledge.

"When will we meet him?" I asked.

"Very soon," Boris said, with a laugh.

"But even three people isn't a movement," I argued.

"Many now understand how badly change is needed. And where persuasion fails, a well-aimed bullet will succeed with a whip and club to insure order.

"Away with the atheism of traitors and the filth corrupting the young and destroying spirit. Awful deeds that seem pointless can be the most fruitful since their shock places terrific pressure on the government to crack down on even the least defiant. When that happens, anger turns conformists into rebels and social order crumbles. Then comes The Day," Boris said passionately.

While speaking, he rose from the bed to stalk the room, jabbing a finger like a prophet as the sweat of emotion trickled down his face. I listened with fascination to the bill of particulars: the seizure of high offices by traitors; the hoard of weapons which would not just rust.

His readiness to murder for the sake of that vision was the madness of a fiend seeing devils menacing him from every corner. From the pocket of his robe, he thrust a brown leather address book in my face. "We're far from alone. Nearly twenty officials await The Day!" he cried, before falling on the bed in a drunken stupor after revealing his plan.

Aided by her American contact, Page and I would assassinate an American official in Washington. After evidence of Russian complicity was discovered, Russia's President would be killed or ousted, leaving the post open for Boris. This plan *might* succeed, if not starting a nuclear war between America and Russia of course.

Boris was cunning, having led the other conspirators as the power behind the throne. His group was like a poisonous snake. Chop off a piece of its tail and you're dead before the second strike. But knowing the plotters, it could be destroyed.

My resolve stiffened grew as Boris lay snoring. The video he showed us that evening had assured it. Patience is not always a virtue, Borya once told me.

Chapter 144

The video he showed was of a Radical Islamic terrorist atrocity. It vividly portrayed a man's tortured death. Thankfully, Boris had lowered the volume.

The camera was mounted high with the nighttime scene being brightly lit. The ground was a large flat rock fitted with an iron ring at each corner. A naked bearded man was bound to the rings. He lay on his back with his eyes closed, screaming mouth open, and head thrashing from side to side.

A figure slipped a towel under the captive's head to keep him from knocking himself out. This person then squatted beside him holding a knife, checking the camera's angle to not obstruct its view. He pressed the tip of the blade half-way between the man's groin and navel, causing blood to well from within.

The blade moved up the man's stomach with blood chasing it all the way. The killer then pressed his finger within, sliding it up and down. Rooting up to his wrists in the exposed stomach until laying glittering intestines on the shrieking man's chest.

Page and I had sat stunned, speechless.

"Why did they do it?" I finally asked.

"That's what traitors deserve," Boris said flatly, as if this explained.

The video had replayed through my mind as I watched Boris snore. I dressed quickly and packed my belongings in my overnight bag. Without further thought I removed my silent pistol from its hiding place.

Chapter 145

Shooting a person isn't like shooting a paper target. Unless the killer is completely crazy, it comes with a crippling emotional reaction even if there is no choice like when a soldier must kill or be killed. The prospect of dying simplified my thinking. Were Boris awake and aware of my true identity, he would instantly kill me.

My action would bear no legal consequence. Boris' death would prevent a bloody civil war and possible nuclear exchange between Russia and America. Even just the heightened international tension could be perilous. Missile exchanges had been barely avoided during the Cold War.

Borya told me that he didn't burden his agents with detailed instructions. Give them a mission and let them sink or swim was his policy. When I said this must use up a lot of agents he declared that he tried "to pick individuals who are survivors." "How do you know a survivor?" I asked. "If they return I know," he said. I will be one, I told myself.

Standing distant enough to avoid blood spatter, I pointed the pistol at Boris' temple and pulled the trigger.

The sound was like a soft clap, not as quiet as in movies but unheard outside the room's thick walls.

Boris' body shuddered and then relaxed. I had been taught to shoot twice ("a double tap") and did though it was visibly unnecessary. I considered crafting a suicide setup by placing the gun in Boris' hand but this was impossible. No one ever shot themselves *twice* in the head.

With the hope of avoiding another killing, I opened the door and heard no sound. Page was likely in a drunken sleep and Boris had no live-in staff. I didn't spend time searching for surveillance cameras. Their tapes wouldn't matter since any police investigation would be perfunctory. There would be no inquest and burial would be quick. The President might send flowers to Boris' memorial service but likely wouldn't attend.

I sneaked from the silent apartment into the empty elevator and outside. The wind was cold but I felt nothing.

Chapter 146

Across from the apartment building was a small, deserted park. There, I sat on a bench and phoned Borya. I had been given two phone numbers: one would be answered by his chief assistant and the other personally. I was instructed to use the latter only in the gravest emergency. He vowed that it would cause him to rise from his coffin but God help the agent who used it needlessly. Despite the early hour he picked up on the second ring. I didn't use my code name. I couldn't remember it.

"It's Margaret. Boris planned a coup following the assassination of an American politician. Evidence of Russian involvement would be found and Russia's President would be ousted or killed. I have his list of allies," I said.

"Boris?" Borya asked.

"He's dead but the others are out there. I need transport," I said, and told him my location.

"You'll be brought to me. The President must be informed," he said, before abruptly hanging up.

While waiting, I filled my mind with a relaxing thought, almost as chant: it's over and you're going home to James and Donna and Randy.

I stood as five men neared and encircled me. Wearing helmets and armored vests, each carried a submachine gun. Carrying two hand grenades in a tactical waist belt, they were dressed for war. It was obviously me who they sought. No one else was around. The man in the middle spoke.

"You are M1. We are instructed to contact you and take you directly to SVR headquarters. In particular we are not to permit you to be approached by police or military persons," he said in English.

"Lead the way," I said, feeling intensely tired.

Chapter 147

SVR headquarters is located in Yasenevo, a southern suburb of Moscow. The sight of its twenty-one story building assured me that I would not be arrested or killed. One of Borya's assistants met me outside his office door.

"The General is on the phone. You can wait nearby," she said.

She led me to a small suite containing a bar and small refrigerator, comfortable seating, and a bathroom with shower. I dropped my travel bag and plopped on the sofa. Sleep would have been welcome but didn't arrive. After checking for the presence of Boris' address book in my pocket, I reloaded my pistol. Though needless, the action comforted me. It was the classic obsessive behavior of a soldier coming down after a dangerous mission. Mentally, I wasn't all there.

I had just replaced the gun in my pocket when Borya entered the room. The gravity of event was mirrored in his clothing. This was ordinarily a bespoke suit, purchased in London on one of his visits. Now he wore a green military field uniform.

I handed him Boris' list of confederates and said, "You look tired."

"It's early. Few will sleep when they learn," he said.

He scanned the names, exhibiting surprise at some.

"Rest while I speak with the President," he said, and left the room.

Unable to sleep, I rummaged through the refrigerator and bar. Despite the allure of alcohol, I had broken enough Mormon commandments that day and chose the sparkling water. Finding cold-baked salmon, my favorite food, cheered me and I made a thick sandwich on black bread. My healthy appetite surprised me. Borya reappeared as I chewed. He looked harried.

"Things are happening," I said, in a neutral tone.

"Many. Article 101 goes into effect at noon," he said.

Then, in response to my mystified look, he explained.

"It allows for defensive measures when martial law is declared. Military units are being recalled to base and borders closed. To avoid misreading, nations have been told this measure will be brief and is vital for a criminal investigation."

"With all borders closed, I'll be stuck here for the duration," I said, evenly.

"No. You and Gerald must leave the country immediately. Valentina can accompany him if she wishes."

"I'm going home!" I declared, ecstatically.

"You're not ready. Rest for a week to forget. Prague is lovely and uncrowded with tourists this time of year," Borya said.

Though longing for home, I also recognize sensible advice when I hear it.

Chapter 148

While potentially world shattering events took place, our lives were paralyzed by Valentina's indecision. As she and Gerald considered, Alex and I chatted over current events.

"Wasn't it just another power struggle between the Federal Security Service and Volgograd's *siloviki* (network of security and military officials), though more intense as the President's term ends," I said.

"There's anxiety who'll comes out on top," Alex agreed.

"Russia's political intrigues are like bulldogs fighting under the carpet. An outsider hears growls but only knows who won when they see bones fly from beneath," I said.

"You're quoting Winston Churchill," Alex chided.

"A good writer steals only from the best," I said, with a smile.

"It's above my pay grade," Alex said.

"Mine too. When *will* Valentina decide?" I asked, feeling more than a little annoyed.

"Relax. Even a romance movie takes hours," Alex said.

Valentina's decision came too late to catch the last commercial flight. With Borya's help, we flew to Prague on an Antonov An-148 from Moscow's Alabino Air Force base. Being the only passengers on this 100-seat twin-jet, we had plenty of room. Just after take-off, too late to object, I Googled the plane's details and gulped. This model had *two* fatal accidents. One, because the pilot topped the "Never Exceed" speed during an emergency descent killing six crew members on a test flight. The later, still unsolved accident caused the death of all sixty-five passengers and six crew members.

While Gerald and Valentina relaxed in their starry-eyed Paradise, I prayed continually. After landing, I did what I advise my children: Breathe deeply and reboot.

Chapter 149

My break in picturesque Prague turned out fine. Our hotel was the fifty-room Absolutum in the Holesovice District. Lacking the noisy atmosphere of larger hotels, its basics included a wellness center and a full-size sauna imported from Finland. Locally designed décor and artwork were added attractions.

I even found a restaurant to suit my healthy eating style: Bistro 8 with old-time Czech dishes like *bramboracka* (potato soup) and a Moroccan-style vegetable dish. During one meal I saw round, larger-than-life, clip-on, gold button earrings win Valentina's heart. Common in the 1930s and 1940s, they regained status after first lady Jackie Kennedy adopted the style. Gerald inherited these from this grandmother.

"Hoop earrings and multiple piercings will fade like other fads. But worn next to the eyes, these can't be overlooked like other jewelry," Valentina said.

"Except for one with eyes as lovely as yours," Gerald said.

"*Yes*," Valentina said.

MARGARET IN MOSCOW

As Gerald took her hand, I teared-up at their union. Why isn't *my* boyfriend so romantic and sensible? I moaned to myself. Whenever I spoke of marrying, which was certainly reasonable since we had two children, he refused to answer which is the best way of winning an argument that I know of.

Chapter 150

Tactfully recognizing my unwanted status, I considered my life while wandering the city alone. Now I fully accepted Borya's judgment: I *was* emotionally wiped out, not ready to rejoin my family. Though looking normal, I wasn't all there. I needed freedom from the routine stresses on parents, and the extraordinary ones on secret agents too.

For these, Prague was ideal. Its 10th century Old Town Square with baroque buildings and Gothic churches soothed my soul. I explored Europe's oldest Jewish house of worship and the old Jewish Cemetery with its vertically stacked graves.

Equally moving was the memorial to Jan Hus, a Czech church reformer executed in 1415. None would argue with the monument's inscription, taken from a letter he wrote while in prison: "Love one another, wish the truth to everyone."

On my fifth solitary day I discovered the Maitrea vegetarian restaurant next to Old Town Square. It had great food and prices and the management was exceptionally conscientious with dishes being specified as vegan or containing honey or onions or gluten. That day I chose shiitake mushroom pate, almonds and seeds with plum sauce, and toasted bread.

The restaurant was crowded and, while busily stuffing myself, a waiter interrupted. He asked if another customer could join my table and I agreed.

Chapter 151

After seating himself, the stranger gave his order to the hovering waiter (chicken soy roll filled with feta cheese and tomatoes) before turning to me.

"I apologize for disturbing you," he said, in accented English with a shy smile.

"You're not. I was just thinking about life," I said.

I might have said, "you're not," or replied with a smile and returned attention to my food. That I didn't, I later realized, indicated my need for company after days of solitude.

"Life's daily task is to create order from chaos," he said, still retaining his smile.

I agreed after taking time to digest this weighty statement.

"That explains everything," I said.

"And nothing," he added.

His deprecating laugh caused me to like him immediately. The man was tall and agile with an exact age that was difficult to determine. With his bright eyes, firm mouth and chin, and air of picture-perfect mental and physical health, he is probably in his forties, I decided. He seemed to be one who lived with pride and serenity but an underlying seriousness too.

I returned to my food, feeling unsure how much to reveal. While traveling, people often share intimate facts with strangers, considering this safe since they won't meet again. I knew better and hesitated.

"Are you a student?" he asked.

Feeling delight since this implied youth rather than the old harried mother that I occasionally thought myself, I told him the truth.

"Bless you for the compliment, but no. I'm here to relax from my three-year-old twins in America. Are you French?" I asked.

"You've noted the accent. I adopt it in restaurants to get better service," he confessed.

Chapter 152

Between bites, I studied my companion. Despite the accent, he seemed as American as Mom's apple pie, like a hand-picked agent of the FBI.

"What do you do?" I asked.

"I'm retired but free-lance to keep myself busy," he said.

"I've been called nosy but didn't ask first," I said, with a smile.

"Vocation seems the first question of all Americans. They pigeon-hole strangers by job more than other nationals."

"Maybe to save time, to see if the other person is worth their interest."

"Am I?" he asked.

"If I *were* free you definitely would, though being several years older," I said.

My mock-serious tone produced another of his charming laughs. What about him makes me so friendly? I wondered, as we returned attention to food.

To end the romantically tinged aura of our chat I changed the subject.

"My father was a lawyer before becoming a judge," I said.

"Judges can see themselves as God-like. Did the change of career affect him?" he asked.

"No, but his friends became edgy as if fearing they'd be jailed for saying something wrong," I said.

"I've had that worry too."

"As a lawyer in court?" I asked.

"No," he replied.

"You weren't accidentally seated at my table, were you?" I asked, after several moments of thinking.

"No, I waited. You were later than usual today," he said.

My mind raced. The sharp knife that I held made an excellent weapon. I could kill him and walk casually from the restaurant, like in the scene from *The Godfather* movie. Customers would focus on his falling body and not me. I would contact Borya for help.

The stranger stiffened and nodded toward the knife.

MARGARET IN MOSCOW

"Lucifer sent me. You won't need that," he said.

Chapter 153

I relaxed and dropped the knife. Lucifer (The Devil) was Borya's nickname, denoting his craftiness.

"He wouldn't let you be unguarded. You've been watched since arriving in Prague. I live here and was asked to assist. I'm Josef," he said.

"I'm pleased to meet you, Josef," I said, extending a hand.

His handshake was firm but not painful.

"I didn't intend for us to meet but became uneasy. You seemed oblivious to your surroundings," Josef said.

"I have been. You know what happened?" I asked.

"From my father. He's clued-in with the President and learns everything."

I made a quizzical look.

"He manages to choose the right side," Josef added.

"There would be no wars if men knew the winner," I said.

"My father did well," Josef said.

His father being a super-rich oligarch explains why this obviously healthy man could retire so young, I thought.

"How are you doing?" Josef unexpectedly asked.

I replied honestly, needing a friend and believing he would understand.

"Not well. The demons come at night. I see faces, first living and then twisted with the mask of death. I fall asleep as dawn leaks through the window, later dressing and trying to act normal," I said.

"It'll get better. It's good you're on vacation," Josef said.

I smiled faintly, knowing that his prophecy was but a hope.

"From your mouth to God's ear," I said.

Bow we both smiled.

Chapter 154

Having Josef as companion, I *did* get better. Once, when we joined Gerald and Valentina for dinner, I introduced him as local who I met at a restaurant, adding that his father was an intimate of Russia's President lest they worry.

As we became close, I teasingly called him "my favorite spy."

"Not a spy, a *Case Officer*," he chided with mock irritation.

"A Case Officer sits at a desk and doesn't protect agents in the field," I objected.

I wasn't annoyed but fishing for information, having become bored with inaction.

"You're no longer depressed," Josef accurately observed.

"It's time for me to return to the fray," I said.

"Your children are young and need you. Go to them," Josef said.

Then, recognizing that he might have spoken too directly, he went on.

"My mother died when I was seven and I still miss her. We talk in my dreams and she holds me. She tells me to marry again and have children. My wife was killed by my father's enemy as a lesson. Borya had him killed," Josef said.

He showed me photos of his dead wife and mother. Both were finely-featured and beautiful. His next statement startled me.

"Borya has found me a wife," Josef said.

I knew that arranged marriages exist in some cultures but it astonished me that Borya had taken such a personal interest.

"Do you favor your proposed wife?" I asked.

"Certainly. She's very beautiful," Josef said.

With this, he passed over a photo from his wallet. I stared and remained open-mouthed. The picture was of Page.

Chapter 155

Josef gushed like a smitten schoolgirl after her first date.

"She's much younger than me but says it doesn't matter. It's how you think that does and that I think young. Her parents and brothers died in a car accident. They were good, moral people and she greatly loved them. It's sad that she'll have no family to celebrate with us," Josef said.

I wondered who created *that* story but said only, "You're very fortunate."

"Yes. Borya introduced her to my father who already loves her. Borya will be godfather to our first child."

Hearing this caused me to choke on my swallowed water.

"Are you all right?" Josef asked, with concern.

"Absolutely!" I sputtered with feigned sincerity. "It's a fairy-tale: Heaven has sent you an angel to love. Have you set the date?" I asked.

MARGARET IN MOSCOW

"My father said I shouldn't let her get away. The wedding is in three days, here at the Russian Consulate. Borya will attend and wishes your presence," Josef said.

"I'd be honored," I said.

I had been worrying about Page since Russia's penalty for treason is a bullet in the head. Why was her life spared? I wondered. Despite her being a moral idiot, I liked Page. She had also been revolted by Boris' video. She might make a good wife if she could keep her stories straight.

Josef nodded for the bill and we left the restaurant. It had been a memorable hour.

Chapter 156

Page's and Josef's wedding consisted of hasty government vows. Not what mothers want for their children but this didn't matter to the couple.

Page was different. Though her beauty and criminally thin body couldn't be hidden, she had toned down her appearance. Instead of a skin-hugging outfit and larger-than-life make-up, she wore the palest lipstick and an ankle-length dress suitable for a nun.

Her attitude was changed too. The brashness was gone and she spoke little. When questioned, she looked toward Josef before answering as if seeking his permission to reply.

"I'm very pleased to meet you," I quickly said when we met.

"It's good that you could join us on this festive day," she replied, with a smile that suggested no acquaintance.

After the ceremony we adjoined to a neighboring room where a buffet had been set. Students of the Russian Academy of National Economy and Public Administration, in Prague for their practical training, passed us in the hallway after meeting with diplomats. Josef impulsively invited them to join our celebration and, after brief hesitation, they agreed. Though of college age, their behavior remained subdued. Despite Borya's cheery welcome, he radiated authority.

Borya knew the Ambassador from international conferences which both attended. They had much to share and it took a while before I got Borya alone.

"I worried what happened to Page," I said in a low tone.

"Why?" Borya asked.

"Russian traitors are usually shot," I declared.

Borya looked at me with surprise.

"My sweet child, you are naïve. Page is a gifted agent. A broken tool is fixed, not discarded. Josef will give her the firmness and close watch that she needs and motherhood will change her. She was told that if she is not pregnant within a year, her future will be reevaluated. Advise her as only a close friend can."

So I did.

Chapter 157

Borya's request had surprised me since Page must hate me. I had used our friendship to betray her, lost her a fortune, and jeopardized her life. And disregard that my actions might also have prevented nuclear war since narcissists aren't known for their objectivity. How would she behave when we met?

Borya arranged our meeting in an empty office at the consulate. They were talking when I entered and he immediately left. Silence continued until I spoke.

"I understand why you must hate me," I said, softly.

Her response wasn't the fury that I expected. Instead, she said tearfully, "You were the only real friend I ever had."

"I still am. Being Borya's agent didn't mean that I lacked feelings. You've had a hard life and didn't have much choice," I said.

While this didn't forgive her deeds it was true. After experiencing brutal childhood abuse, she had turned to a life of crime. Yet, as indicated by her interest in Wicca, perhaps yearned for goodness too. *"Let they who are without sin cast the first stone..."*

To change the subject I said, "I'm a mother with three-year-old twins in America."

"I need to become pregnant," Page said, fervently.

"You will."

"The doctor said I'm healthy. Borya insisted on my medical exam before..."

I simply nodded. The forced marriage and Borya's demand she become pregnant were delicate issues.

"Josef is a good man. He was told a fairy tale and knows nothing of my past," Page said.

"Keep it that way, and a bit of advice. My mother told me that when she wants something important she simply drops a hint. My father later agrees, believing that it was his idea," I said.

"I've known many men but still have a lot to learn," Page said demurely.

"That's what friends are for," I said, taking her hand.

Chapter 158

A few minutes later, the students expressed thanks and exited the reception, the bride and bridegroom departed on their honeymoon, and Gerald and Valentina left too. Borya, Alex, and I relaxed after the tumultuous weeks.

"Is it over?" I asked, wearily.

"Almost. The few still in hiding will be found, martial law has ended, and the borders are open with things are back to normal. There's just one more matter," Borya said.

I sprawled, feeling exhausted and looking it, fearing a new assignment.

Unhurriedly, Borya filled wine glasses. Raising his, he toasted, "To Margaret of America From the People of Russia: *Dolgaya Zhizn'i Zdorov'ye!*" (Long Life and Health). I sobbed in his arms.

Borya's duties kept him in Moscow but Alex accompanied me home. Upon landing at Newark Airport, I remembered that I hadn't brought presents for my children as promised. Mothering concerns kicked in and I involved Alex in the search.

"I don't want one-and-done toys with flashy screens and fake school questions. I want flexible things that last and with which they can create and interact with their world," I said.

"Sounds good but buy a lot. Kids always think that more is better," Alex said.

I was surprised by her respectable insight which I, a mother, hadn't thought of. Instead of going directly to Greenwich, we first traveled into Manhattan to scour Macy's toy department, finally choosing large-piece floor puzzles, a colorful Wooden Rainbow with which to create tunnels and ramps, Superhero Capes for dress-up play, and a Hungry Hungry Hippo board game. With these in the limousine's trunk, I buckled my seat-belt and turned toward Alex.

"*Now* I can go home," I said.

Chapter 159

Because of the crush of events, I hadn't phoned my family in days and felt guilt and fear. Parenthood carries this in spades, I thought, as I dialed home. When there was no answer after ten rings I really worried: the voice mail was set to pick up after four!

"What's wrong?" Alex asked, noting my expression.

"I don't know. No one's home and the voicemail didn't pick up as it should," I said slowly.

Then, phoning my parents, I heard not my mother's voice but her cheery voicemail greeting.

"Something's wrong," I exclaimed.

Scenarios raced through my mind: Boris' allies had discovered my true identity, murdered my family for revenge and awaited me; fatal illness; a gas line explosion had ravaged all. I babbled these fears and Alex touched my hand as I had comforted Page.

"You're overly tired and not thinking clearly. The only ones knowing your identity are those who should.

It's probably something ordinary like being out," Alex said, reassuringly.

Regaining my wits, I punched in Mila's phone number. After her assignment as my family's bodyguard, she quickly became a friend and emergency babysitter. She picked up on the first ring.

"I called and called but no one answered. Where is everybody?" I screamed.

"Margaret?"

"Yes. I'm sorry. I'm worried," I said, apologetically.

"They're at Randy's parents' house celebrating his graduation. Where are you?" Mila asked.

Tears of relief rolled down my cheeks as I spoke.

"I'm on the Thruway, on my way," I said.

"They're partying my boyfriend's graduation. All's okay," I told Alex.

She hugged me until the sobbing stopped.

Chapter 160

Randy reached me first, my toddlers quickly followed, and I entered the house clung to all. None knew where I had been and feared the worst. Alex dismissed the driver and carried in the toys which were ignored. They will love them later, I thought.

I introduced Alex as my friend from Moscow, no longer needing to keep secret where I had been. In the internet age, yesterday's events are old news and the coup attempt in Russia was already ancient. Its American connection would have kept it alive but this wasn't made public.

"You made it!" I told Randy, though no one had ever doubted his graduation.

"And more. A hedge fund is funding my idea. We're set," he said, exuberantly.

"Whatever makes you happy," I said.

We already had enough money to support a comfortable lifestyle but two issues remained: our marriage, and my persuading him of the more babies that I wanted. He wasn't yet ready but age is more important for women in this regard. Our clinging toddlers prevented intimate conversation and we babbled with them as if the rest of the world didn't exist.

With my safe arrival, the others relaxed. Mila spoke animatedly with Alex in Russian and Randy's father and mine held forth. Lawyers and doctors yearn for a pulpit and my father is a judge and Randy's is a surgeon.

This celebration was also to announce the engagement of my oldest sister, Melody, to a young doctor. His calm face concealed recent suffering: having been made party to a lawsuit merely from, during his training, observed in another doctor's office. The insurance company had just settled the case.

I unwrapped the toys, leaving them for James and Donna to explore. My talk with Randy about *the* issue was long overdue.

Chapter 161

Grasping Randy by the hand, I took us to his bedroom. Seating myself on the desk chair, I pointed him toward the bed to indicate my disinterest in love-making. He sat compliantly and raised the issue first.

"You want us to get married," he said.

"Only if you do too. It would be sensible and I won't wait forever. We've dated since high school and have two kids. Well?" I said.

"I was waiting for you to propose," Randy said, light-heartedly.

I didn't join his smile, it not being the time for humor.

"*Well*?" I repeated, sternly.

Randy didn't answer immediately. I sensed that he wasn't fully committed but also that he didn't want to lose me.

"It is past time but I do have one demand," he said finally.

"What is it?"

"That you never lie to me. You don't have to tell me about your work. I trust it'll be honorable but promise that you'll never lie to me. Never ever, not a single time for any reason," Randy said.

"*I'll never lie to you,*" I said slowly.

"Are we having a religious wedding?" he asked, after a momentary silence.

Being irreligious, I knew Randy wouldn't feel comfortable with one.

"No. You won't become Mormon or they approve having our kids as ring-bearers. The religion is old-fashioned that way," I said.

Randy left the bed and lifted me into his arms.

"Set the date," he said firmly.